HARPERCOLLINS CHILDREN'S

Stories
for

5

Year Olds

HARPERCOLLINS CHILDREN'S

Stories for 5

Year Olds

Compiled by Julia Eccleshare

HarperCollins *Children's Books*

First published in the United Kingdom by HarperCollins, Young Lions, in 1991 as
Big Beans or Little Beans? and Other Stories for Five-Year-Olds
Published in this revised edition by HarperCollins *Children's Books* in 2022
HarperCollins *Children's Books* is a division of HarperCollins*Publishers* Ltd
1 London Bridge Street
London SE1 9GF

www.harpercollins.co.uk

HarperCollins*Publishers*
Macken House, 39/40 Mayor Street Upper
Dublin 1, D01 C9W8, Ireland

2

ISBN 978-0-00-852467-8

The authors and illustrators assert the moral right to be identified
as the authors and illustrators of the work respectively.

A CIP catalogue record for this title is available from the British Library.

Typeset in 13/24pt ITC Century Std by Palimpsest Book Production Ltd,
Falkirk, Stirlingshire

Printed and bound in the UK using 100% renewable
electricity at CPI Group (UK) Ltd

This book is produced from independently certified FSC™ paper
to ensure responsible forest management.

Find out more about HarperCollins and the environment at
www.harpercollins.co.uk/green

Contents

Mr Curry's Birthday Treat

Michael Bond
Illustrated by R. W. Alley

Early one spring morning Paddington hurried into the garden as soon as he had finished breakfast in order to inspect his rockery. He was an optimistic bear at heart, and having planted some seeds the day before, he was looking forward to seeing the results.

The seeds had been a free gift in one of Mrs Brown's magazines, and the picture on the side of the packet was a blaze of bright yellow flowers. Some of them were almost as tall as the magazine's gardening expert, Alf Greenways.

Mr Greenways was known to his many friends in the trade as 'Beanpole Greenways', so it was as good a recommendation for success as anyone could possibly wish for.

He also owned the nursery supplying the sunflower seeds, so it was no wonder he was beaming all over his face as he held a watering can aloft, spurring his blooms to even greater heights.

Paddington got down on all fours and peered at the freshly raked soil in his patch of garden, but apart from a disconsolate-looking caterpillar, there wasn't so much as the tiniest of green shoots to be seen. Everything was exactly as he had left it the night before when he had gone outside with a torch before going to bed.

Mr Greenway's seeds were rather large and he couldn't help wondering if he had planted them upside down by mistake.

A robin redbreast landed on a nearby rock to take a closer look at what was going on, but having spotted Paddington's network of cotton threads protecting the patch, it flew off in disgust.

Mr Brown was right. Gardens were a good example of life in the raw; a constant battle between good and evil. Slugs, for example, were given very short shrift, often ending up with the contents of a salt cellar upended over them, whereas worms were always welcome – unless of course they happened to come up for air in the middle of the lawn.

All the same, it was disappointing, and for a moment or two Paddington toyed with the idea of going indoors and fetching his binoculars in case the caterpillar had a hearty appetite and he could see traces of green on its lips.

He was in the middle of weighing up the pros and cons when he heard an all-too-familiar voice calling out to him.

His heart sank as he looked up and saw the Browns' neighbour peering at him over the top of the fence. Not that there was anything new in that; Mr Curry was a notorious busybody and he spent his life poking his nose into other people's affairs.

Because his patch of garden coincided with some higher ground on Mr Curry's side, Paddington often bore the brunt.

It was most disappointing. Mr Brown had spent half of the weekend raising the fence at that particular point, with the express intention of putting a stop to their neighbour's spying.

At the time Mrs Bird had said 'the chance would be a fine thing' and it looked as though her worst fears were being realised.

'What are you doing, bear?' growled Mr Curry suspiciously. 'Up to no good as usual, I suppose.'

'Oh, no, Mr Curry,' said Paddington. 'I was just checking my blooms – except I haven't got any yet. Mrs Bird was right. She said you would be bound to find a box to stand on. I mean . . .'

'What was that, bear?' barked Mr Curry.

'Mrs Bird saw a fox in our garden the other day,' said Paddington hastily. 'She thinks it came over here because it couldn't find anything interesting in yours.'

Paddington was normally the most truthful of bears and he stayed where he was for a moment or two in case the proverbial thunderbolt landed on his head, but nothing happened, so he breathed a sigh of relief and carried on looking for new plant shoots.

'I don't see any point in having flowers,' growled Mr Curry. 'Nasty things. They make the place untidy – dropping their petals everywhere. Just you wait.'

'I was hoping Mr Brown might take a photograph of mine when they are ready,' explained Paddington. 'It's my Aunt Lucy's birthday in August and she says flowers always brighten things up. They don't have many in the Home for Retired Bears in Lima and I thought I could send her a picture she can keep by her bed.'

A gleam entered Mr Curry's eyes and he suddenly perked up. 'Do you know what day it is today, bear?' he asked casually.

Paddington thought for a moment. 'I think it's a Wednesday, Mr Curry,' he said.

'Nothing else about it?' asked Mr Curry.

'Not that I know of,' said Paddington. 'I can ask Mrs Bird if you like.'

'I don't think that will be necessary,' said Mr Curry hastily. Reaching inside his jacket pocket, he removed a folded sheet of paper.

'It's funny you should mention the word "birthday", bear,' he continued, waving it in the air. 'Quite a coincidence, in fact. Don't tell anyone else, but it happens to be my birthday today.'

'Does it really, Mr Curry?' exclaimed Paddington. 'I didn't know that.'

'Well,' said the Browns' neighbour, 'you do now, but since you have clearly forgotten the fact, it's . . .'

He broke off as the paper slipped from his fingers and they both watched it flutter to the ground on Paddington's side of the fence and land at his feet.

'Now look what you've made me do!' he barked. 'I've dropped my list of presents . . . I sat up late last night making it out . . .'

Paddington looked shocked. 'You haven't

opened them already have you, Mr Curry?' he exclaimed. 'Mrs Bird says that's supposed to be very unlucky.'

'I don't have any to open yet, bear,' said Mr Curry. 'That paper you made me drop contains a list of all the things I wouldn't mind having.

'I made it out in case anyone happens to be stuck for ideas,' he added casually.

Paddington made haste to retrieve the paper. From a quick glance, it seemed to be rather long.

'Don't bother reading it now, bear,' said Mr Curry hastily. 'You can keep it to browse over at your leisure. However, there isn't much time left, so I suggest you don't hang about. I wouldn't want you to be disappointed.'

'Thank you very much, Mr Curry,' said

Paddington doubtfully. 'Bears are good at browsing, so I don't expect I shall keep it very long.'

But the Browns' neighbour had already disappeared. One moment he was there, the next moment, following what sounded remarkably like a chuckle, his kitchen door slammed shut.

Paddington stood where he was for a moment or two, wondering what to do with the paper in his paw; then he slowly made his way back to the kitchen.

Mrs Bird, the Browns' housekeeper, was busy making marmalade, but she gave one of her snorts when he told her what had happened. 'I'll give that Mr Curry a birthday present,' she said.

Withdrawing a wooden spoon from one of

the saucepans, she licked it with evident relish. 'One he won't forget in a hurry.'

Catching sight of an anxious look on Paddington's face, she softened. 'I daresay he can't help being the way he is. He must have been born that way. It's our bad luck we have the misfortune to live next door to him.

'It isn't like me to forget anyone's birthday,' she continued, her mind clearly on other things. 'Even Mr Curry's. I thought it was much later in the year . . .

'Could you read out some of the things he wants – I daren't leave my saucepans for a moment in case they boil over.'

Paddington was only too pleased to oblige.

'A new ballcock for the cistern . . .' he announced, '. . . a mouse trap . . . breakfast cereal (see two packets for price of one offer at cut-price grocers) . . . a three-for-one offer on tubes of shaving cream from new stall in market . . .'

'I take it all back,' said Mrs Bird, over another quick stir. 'He must have turned over a new leaf. It doesn't sound like him at all. It's much too modest.'

She thought for a moment. 'It just so happens I have a fruit cake in the oven. It was meant for our tea, but it won't take long to cover it with marzipan . . . he likes lots of candles and his name written in the icing . . .

'It would happen today when I'm up to my eyes. It's way past the marmalade-making season, but I'm experimenting with some Seville oranges I've been keeping in the freezer. I'm not too sure how they will turn out.'

'Your 2009s were very good, Mrs Bird,' said Paddington knowledgeably. 'I stuck three of the labels from the jars into my scrapbook to remind me. It was the best I've ever had.'

'All gone, I'm afraid,' said Mrs Bird, hiding her pleasure as best she could over the saucepan. 'And there's not much left of the 2010s either. I don't know what happens to marmalade in this house,' she added meaningly. 'It just disappears.'

Clearly in two minds about what to do next, she began sorting out her spoons.

'Perhaps I could help, Mrs Bird?' said Paddington. 'I wouldn't want your experiment to go wrong.'

'Would you mind, dear?' said Mrs Bird. 'You could get him some of that shaving cream.' Reaching into her handbag she withdrew a five pound note. 'That ought to take care of it.'

Paddington needed no second bidding. The steam from the saucepan was making his whiskers droop, and with Mrs Brown at the hairdressers, and both Jonathan and Judy away at school, he was at a bit of a loose end, so he was on his way in no time at all.

Over the years he had become a well-known figure in the Portobello market, and although he had gained a reputation for driving a hard bargain, the resident traders were always pleased to see him.

That said, more often than not, outsiders

with their barrows were a case of 'here today and gone tomorrow', so it was some while before Paddington came across the one he was looking for.

Chalked on a large piece of slate were the words: TODAY'S BARGAIN, and underneath a smaller announcement that said: THREE ORDINARY SIZE TUBES OF SHAVING CREAM ALL IN ONE GIANT TUBE!

'As used by some of the crowned 'eads of Europe in the old days,' called the stall keeper, rubbing his hands in anticipation of a sale as he saw Paddington eyeing his display. 'It wasn't my fault it fell off the back of a lorry a couple of days ago just as I 'appened to be setting up me barrow. I ran after it, but it was gone before I could say 'alf a mo.'

He took a closer look at Paddington. 'If

24

you don't mind my saying so,' he said. 'You look as though you could do with a good shave . . .

'I'm not asking two nicker. I'm not even asking three. Seeing as you're the first customer of the day, you can 'ave one of them giant tubes for four pounds . . .'

Paddington gave the man a hard stare. 'Aren't you going the wrong way?' he said, raising his hat politely.

The stall keeper paused and his eyes narrowed. 'I can see there are no flies on you, mate,' he said. 'If you don't fancy 'aving a good shave, how about a new titfer tat?' He reached out for a pile of hats. 'Yours looks as if it's seen better days.'

'It belonged to my uncle in Darkest Peru,' said Paddington. 'It was handed down. The shaving cream is a birthday present for our next door neighbour.'

Wilting under Paddington's gaze, the man hastily changed his tune. 'Nothing like starting the day with a bit of friendly banter,' he said. 'You can 'ave it for two pounds and seeing it's a birthday present I'll throw in some wrapping paper for luck.'

'Thank you very much,' said Paddington. 'I might come here to do some shopping again tomorrow.'

'I might not be 'ere tomorrow,' said the man with feeling. 'Especially if I get too many customers like you,' he added under his breath.

But Paddington was already on his way.

Even if the wrapping paper did look as though it had seen better days, he still thought it was the best morning's shopping he had done for a long while, and he hurried back to number thirty-two Windsor Gardens as fast as his legs would carry him in order to break the news to Mrs Bird and give her the change from her five pound note.

The Browns' housekeeper could hardly believe her eyes when she saw what Paddington had bought. 'I've never seen such a big tube,' she said. 'I do hope you haven't been taken for a ride. Even bears don't get something for nothing these days.'

'The man said it was the same as some of the crowned heads of Europe used in the old days,' said Paddington.

'That's as may be,' said Mrs Bird. 'But as I recall, most of them had beards, so there can't have been much demand for it.'

'Perhaps that's why they had a lot left over,' said Paddington.

'Perhaps,' said Mrs Bird. It sounded like typical salesman's patter to her, but she didn't want to be a wet blanket.

However, her words weighed heavily on Paddington's mind as he made his way upstairs to his bedroom.

Removing the tube from its box, he examined it carefully. There was no sign of a dent, but if it really had fallen off the back of a lorry it might well have become bent.

To make doubly sure all was well, he fetched Mr Brown's special shaving mirror on a stand from the bathroom. Although one side of the glass was just like an ordinary mirror – the other side made things seem much larger than they really were and that was the one he wanted.

Placing the stand carefully in the centre of his bedside table, he laid his old leather suitcase flat on the floor in front of it and picked up Mr Curry's present.

Having climbed on top of the case, he carefully unscrewed the cap on the end of the tube and held the nozzle up to the mirror before giving the tube itself a gentle squeeze.

A tiny white blob the size of a small pea appeared momentarily, then went back inside again.

Paddington stared at the nozzle. Disappearing shaving cream wouldn't be a good start to anyone's day if they were in a hurry. In his mind's eye he could already hear cries of, 'Bear! Where are you, bear?' issuing from Mr Curry's bathroom window.

Knowing the Browns' neighbour of old, he would be demanding his money back even though he hadn't paid for it.

Bracing himself, Paddington gritted his teeth and had another go. This time he used both paws and gave the tube a much harder squeeze.

For a moment or two nothing happened and he was about to give up when he felt a minor explosion in his paw and a stream of white foamy liquid shot everywhere. It left Mr Brown's mirror looking as though it had been buried by a major blizzard at the North Pole.

Paddington was so taken by surprise he let go of the tube like a hot cake and hovered to and fro on top of his suitcase before finally losing his balance.

Stepping backwards into space, it could only have been a split second or so before he landed on the floor, but the tube had beaten him to it.

As he lay where he had fallen, his legs and arms waving helplessly in the air, he was aware of a further eruption, and through half-closed eyes he saw what remained of the tube's contents flying in all directions.

The largest lump of all hit the ceiling right above his head, and as it slowly detached itself, Paddington jumped to his feet.

He gazed mournfully round the room. It was a long time since he had seen it in quite such a mess, and it had all come about in the twinkling of an eye; so fast, in fact, there was nothing he could possibly have done to stop it.

Hastily returning Mr Brown's mirror to the bathroom before anything else untoward happened, Paddington held it under the tap for a while before returning it to its rightful place.

It took rather longer than he had bargained for, because the hot water made the cream turn into foam and he was soon enveloped in bubbles. That was another thing about messes; they tended to spread, and the more you tried to put things right the worse they became.

It was while he was drying everything as best he could with the towels that his gaze alighted on a wall cabinet above the basin. He knew from past explorations that it was full of interesting things in bottles and packets, but apart from a small spoon and some nail files, he couldn't remember there being any other likely tools. All the same, he took them back to his bedroom, just in case.

Once there, he consulted the instructions on the side of the tube. There was a great deal on the subject of what a wonderful shaving experience lay in wait for the user, but there was nothing at all about how to get the cream back into the tube if too much had come out.

Removing as much as he could from the walls and the furniture before getting down to work, Paddington soon discovered it wasn't as easy as he had expected.

Holding the tube with one paw and applying shaving cream to the nozzle with the spoon, he couldn't help but grip the tube so tightly to stop it bending that in the end most of the cream landed on the floor.

His friend, Mr Gruber, often said that what comes out doesn't necessarily go back in again, and the wisdom of his words was soon confirmed.

In fact, Paddington was concentrating so much on the task in hand he didn't hear Mrs Bird until she was outside his room.

'How are you getting on with wrapping Mr Curry's present?' she called.

'I haven't even started on that, Mrs Bird,' said Paddington.

Opening the door as little as possible, he peered through the gap.

'Do you have to do it in your bedroom?' asked Mrs Bird.

'I do now,' said Paddington sadly.

'Well, let me know if you need a hand with the knots,' said Mrs Bird. 'I shan't be long. I've run out of candles for Mr Curry's cake, and I don't doubt he'll be counting them. I'd better make sure I use enough or that'll be wrong. On the other hand, I don't want to use too many and risk him catching the house on fire.

'I haven't even started on the lettering yet. If anyone phones, tell them I shall be back in a quarter of an hour or so.'

Mrs Bird sounded flustered, as well she might with all that was going on, but after a short pause, Paddington heard the sound of the front door closing and as it did, so it triggered off another of his ideas.

Hurrying downstairs, he made his way to

the kitchen and there, sure enough, lay the answer to his problem. Mr Curry's freshly iced cake was sitting in the middle of the table, and alongside it was exactly what he needed: a canvas bag on the end of which there was a tiny metal funnel. It must have been meant.

'I think,' said Mr Brown, over tea in the garden the following week, 'my handiwork with the fence must have paid off. I haven't seen old Curry looking over it for ages.'

'I'm afraid it's a bit more complicated than that, Henry,' replied Mrs Brown. 'It's all to do with his birthday.'

'If I hadn't been in such a rush the morning after Paddington planted his seeds, I wouldn't have stopped him in the middle of what Mr

Curry said was a list of the presents he wanted,' agreed Mrs Bird.

'When I had the chance to take a proper look it had things on it like a tin of peas . . .'

'And half a cabbage!' added Paddington indignantly. 'It was his shopping list, and we bought him a present too!'

'Hold on a minute,' said Mr Brown. 'What has all that got to do with the garden fence?'

'He dropped the list over our side of the fence . . .' explained Mrs Brown.

'Accidentally on purpose,' broke in Mrs Bird. 'It happened to land at Paddington's feet and Mr Curry said it was his birthday list.'

'In that case he deserves all he got!' said Mr Brown, rising to Paddington's defence. 'Er . . . what did we give him in the end?'

'A tube marked "shaving cream", which was

full of icing sugar,' said Mrs Bird, 'and a cake with his name written across the top in shaving cream. I can't think that either of them went down very well, but it serves him right for playing such a mean trick.'

'I had an accident with the tube,' explained Paddington, 'so I borrowed Mrs Bird's cake-making outfit to get the shaving cream back inside it. Only the bag still had some icing sugar inside it so I put that into the tube by mistake.'

'And when I came to use it,' said Mrs Bird, 'I didn't realise Paddington had filled it with shaving cream. I couldn't think why it wouldn't set.'

'Which, as things turned out,' said Mrs Brown, 'meant that for once Mr Curry couldn't have his cake and eat it too. Perhaps it's taught him a lesson. We haven't had sight nor sound of him since. Let's hope it lasts.'

'Pigs might fly,' snorted Mrs Bird.

'So that's how I came to have traces of shaving cream over my bathroom mirror,' said Mr Brown. 'I thought something must have been going on . . . Hold on a moment,' he continued, as light suddenly dawned. 'Did you say all this happened last Wednesday?'

'I did,' said Mrs Brown. 'Why do you ask, Henry?'

'Because,' said Mr Brown, 'last Wednesday was April the first. You can play any tricks you like before midday. If you ask me, not only was Mr Curry playing an April fool trick, but whoever sold Paddington the shaving cream was probably doing much the same thing.'

'They didn't bargain on the fact that there

are some bears who happen to have been born under a lucky star,' said Mrs Brown. 'Now we are enjoying some peace and quiet for a change, so all's well that ends well.'

And that was something no one could argue with, especially when they saw that seemingly almost overnight Paddington's seeds had begun to sprout. It was nice having things to look forward to.

Cinderella

The Brothers Grimm
Retold by Alison Sage
Illustrated by Sarah Gibb

Once, a long time ago, there lived a girl called Ella. She was as sunny as a summer breeze, and as gorgeous as a field of lilies. Her mother had died when she was a baby, and after many years of living alone, her father married again. Ella's stepmother was pretty to look at, but she was cruel and her two daughters were as unkind as she was.

Doris, the elder, was as silly as she was spiteful. Jezebel, the younger girl, was clever but she was never happier than when she was finding fault with other people.

Both sisters hated Ella from the moment they met.

'Nasty little creep,' said Doris. 'She shan't have any of my clothes.' For her mother gave both daughters anything they wanted, while Ella soon had to make do with old rags.

'Little beast,' said Jezebel. 'Make her sleep in the kitchen.' And that is what happened. Poor Ella was sent to the cold kitchen where she curled up in the cinders to keep warm.

'Look at Cinder-ella!' sneered Jezebel. 'She is just where she belongs.'

The name stuck and it was 'Cinderella, fetch this!' and 'Cinderella, clear that away!' all day long. As the months passed, the two sisters grew more mean and spoiled, but Cinderella was as warm-hearted as ever.

One morning, a letter arrived from the palace. The king was holding a grand ball for the prince to choose a wife. Any girl who thought she could catch his eye was invited. Doris and Jezebel were overcome with excitement. What luck! Each felt sure that she was going to be the one the prince would choose.

'He'll dance with me all night,' daydreamed Doris. 'I'll be in my pink silk with the cream ruffles.'

'You'll look like a raspberry pudding!' jeered Jezebel. 'He'll be dancing with me in my elegant yellow satin with the black lace . . .'

As Cinderella listened to her stepsisters, a tear rolled down her cheek. If only she could go to the ball too! But that was impossible. She was ragged little Cinderella with nothing grand to wear.

What a fuss and flurry followed over the next few days as Jezebel and Doris dithered over what to wear. Cinderella had no peace from morning until night, helping them to squeeze into one hideous outfit after another.

On the evening of the ball the stepsisters were ready at last.

'Don't forget to tidy up while we're gone!' ordered Doris as their carriage swept away down the drive.

Cinderella slipped back to her place in the cinders and cried her heart out. 'I wish I could see the prince!' she sobbed.

All of a sudden, she heard someone calling her name.

'Cinderella! Do stop crying, dear. I'm your fairy godmother.' At Cinderella's side was a beautiful and elegant lady.

'I wish I could go to the ball,' Cinderella whispered through her tears.

'Then go you shall,' said her fairy godmother, smiling as she took out a wand made of stars. 'Get me a pumpkin from the garden. A nice big one.'

Cinderella was so surprised that she did as she was told.

'Now I need four little brown mice,' said her strange visitor. 'Oh – and a fat frog, if you can find one. And two lizards.'

When Cinderella had brought everything

her godmother waved her wand and . . .

Pouff! In a flash of white light a magnificent golden coach appeared with four beautiful horses and a fine coachman. Two footmen leapt smartly up to their places at the back.

'Oh!' cried Cinderella joyfully. But then her face fell. 'What about my dress?'

'Hold still, my dear.' Again her godmother waved her wand in a sparkle of fairy dust.

Cinderella gasped. She was wearing a dress of the purest gold. It glittered in the darkness as if the sun had come out, and Cinderella blinked at its brilliance. Her hair was twined with snowdrops and pearls, and on her feet were the most beautiful golden slippers.

Cinderella's godmother laughed at her amazed face. 'Off you go!' she said kindly. 'But listen. My spell will only last until midnight.

As soon as the clock strikes, all your finery will turn back to rags, so be sure to get home by then.'

'I promise,' said Cinderella and she sprang into the coach and whirled away to the palace.

When Cinderella arrived, the ball was already in full swing and she could hear the sound of music and the happy chatter of the dancers.

She pushed open the great doors and walked into the hall.

There was a gasp of admiration as everyone saw her. The prince, who had been sitting next to his father, leapt to his feet and crossed the hall to take her hand.

Bowing, the prince asked her to dance and as they swept down the long hall he could not take his eyes off her.

'Who can she be?' whispered the ladies.

'She must be a fairy princess,' said the courtiers.

Cinderella had never been so happy. The evening passed in a brilliant blur of laughter and loveliness, the prince always at her side. She spoke kindly to her stepsisters, who didn't recognise her. They blushed with joy to be noticed by the unknown princess.

Cinderella watched the great clock in the hall, counting each precious minute of her time with the prince. She dared not stay too long. At half past eleven, she gave the prince one last smile and slipped away before he realised what was happening.

She ran out of the hall, down the steps and into her coach. And she was gone, leaving the prince desperately searching for her amongst the groups of dancers.

At midnight Cinderella slipped into her old place in the cinders and just as she did so, her dress turned into rags. Four squeaking mice raced across the floor and she knew that her coach was now nothing but a large orange pumpkin.

Soon after, the key rattled in the lock and her stepsisters returned, pink-faced and excited at the wonderful happenings at the ball.

'We made friends with a mystery princess,' said Doris. 'She came and talked to us.'

'Is that so?' murmured Cinderella.

'Yes, I shouldn't wonder if the prince doesn't talk to us next,' said Jezebel. 'There's going to be another ball tomorrow night. The king has invited everyone again.'

'Can I come?' asked Cinderella daringly. 'Don't be stupid,' said Doris.

The next evening, the sisters got ready as before. As the unknown princess had worn a golden dress, they both chose golden dresses too.

Jezebel's sour little face poked out from her gold jewellery like a disagreeable bird. Doris' cheeks shone like lard under a layer of powder.

'Have a good time,' called Cinderella as they set off.

Once again her fairy godmother was there, but this time Cinderella was not weeping. She clapped her hands with delight as her coach magically appeared and, at the touch of a wand, her rags disappeared. They became the most beautiful shell-pink dress, as fine as cobwebs and shimmering with light. Her little shoes were mother-of-pearl and her hair was twined with rosebuds.

Full of thanks, Cinderella sped off to the ball a second time.

'Don't forget to be back before twelve!' called her fairy godmother.

Just as before, the ball had already begun, but the moment she entered the hall, the music stopped. The prince's face, which had been downcast, broke into a wonderful smile and he hurried across the hall to lead her in the next dance.

They talked and talked and afterwards all Cinderella could remember was that they had agreed about everything. They stood quietly watching the dancers when suddenly Cinderella glanced up at the clock. It was quarter to twelve!

She slipped out of the hall, jumped into her coach and away she flew. As the coach was coming up the road towards her house, the clock struck twelve and suddenly she was running home through the darkness in her old rags.

Before long, her sisters came back, chattering excitedly about the ball.

'Was the princess there again tonight?' Cinderella asked them.

'Yes,' frowned Jezebel. 'And the prince wanted to dance with no one but her.'

'But then she disappeared again before he could ask who she was,' said Doris, 'so everyone is going to another ball tomorrow.'

'And we shall wear pink next, so you'd better start getting our things ready,' snarled Jezebel.

On the third night, everything happened as before, except that this time Cinderella's dress was sky blue silk, scattered with diamonds and opals, which flickered like little flames as she moved. On her feet was the most exquisite pair of glass slippers. She looked like a queen.

The prince was waiting for her by the door and the moment she arrived they whirled into a dance.

Then the prince took her hand, and they stood gazing into each other's eyes. Time seemed to stand still and then all of a sudden, Cinderella heard the big clock beginning to strike . . .

Midnight! She flew from the prince's arms

like a startled deer, out of the ballroom and down the great wide steps just as the chimes were finishing. As she ran she dropped one of her little glass slippers.

No one noticed as a girl in rags slipped out of the palace gates and down the road.

Cinderella barely had time to race through the door and sit by the cinders before her stepsisters arrived home.

'What have you been up to?' said Jezebel suspiciously.

'Nothing,' yawned Cinderella. 'Tell me about the princess!'

'You'll never believe it!' said Doris. 'She disappeared again.'

'She dropped a glass slipper,' broke in Jezebel, 'and the king says that whoever it fits will marry the prince.'

The next day, messengers went out to every corner of the kingdom, north, east, south and west, spreading the news. Whoever the shoe fitted would be the royal bride.

'It could be me!' said Doris.

'You!' said Jezebel scornfully.

'That slipper is going to fit me!' And she rubbed her feet with cream to make them smooth and slippery.

Soon the prince arrived.

He hoped that the slipper would not fit either of the sisters, but he offered it to them politely.

They tried . . . and tried. But the harder they pushed, the more their feet bulged out of the little shoe.

'Have you any sisters?' asked the prince.

'Only Cinders,' said Doris spitefully, 'but she doesn't wear shoes at all!'

'Let her try,' said the prince.

So they called for Cinderella who sat down shyly and picked up the little glass slipper.

It fitted perfectly.

And then she put her hand in her pocket and pulled out the other slipper and put that on too.

Doris was too amazed to say a word.

'There must be some mistake!' gasped Jezebel.

'There's no mistake,' smiled the fairy godmother, appearing at that moment. 'This is your princess,' she said to the prince.

'Yes, I know,' he replied, because even in her rags he knew that she was the one.

Cinderella and her prince were married straight away and everyone said that there had never been a lovelier princess, or a more handsome prince.

Cinderella invited all of her family to the wedding and her stepsisters danced with the greatest lords of the land. Her fairy godmother showered Cinderella and the prince with fairy dust, but they hardly noticed because each already had their heart's desire.

Cinderella never forgot her days in rags, and she always had a kind word for everyone, rich or poor. She also could never find it in her heart to chase the mice out of the palace kitchens, or the frogs from the royal pond.

In time, she and her prince became king and queen and ruled their country wisely and well, but their happiness never faded, and nor did their undying love.

Sea Story

Jill Barklem

F or many generations, families of mice have made their homes in the roots and trunks of the trees of Brambly Hedge, a dense and tangled hedgerow that borders the field on the other side of the stream.

The Brambly Hedge mice lead busy lives.

During the fine weather, they collect flowers, fruits, berries and nuts from the Hedge and surrounding fields, and prepare delicious jams, pickles and preserves that are kept safely in the Store Stump for the winter months ahead.

Although the mice work hard, they make time for fun too. All through the year, they mark the seasons with feasts and festivities and, whether it be a little mouse's birthday, an eagerly awaited wedding or the first day of spring, the mice welcome the opportunity to meet and celebrate.

Primrose woke early that summer morning. She dressed quickly and tiptoed down to the kitchen. Her mother was already up, packing a rain cloak and hat into a small bag.

'Off you go,' she said. 'Take this apple to eat on the way. We'll see you later to say goodbye.'

Outside the sun was already warm, and a light breeze stirred the leaves and branches of Brambly Hedge.

'Perfect,' said Primrose, 'just right for an adventure.'

She ran across the field, through the long grass and down to the stream. There she found Dusty, Poppy and Wilfred hard at work, loading provisions on to Dusty's boat.

'Here you are at last,' said Dusty, 'I was beginning to think we'd have to leave you behind.'

Wilfred helped Primrose carry her bag down the steep wooden steps to the cabin below.

'Look at this!' he said, pointing to an

ancient yellow map spread out on the chart table.

'Does it show where we're going?' she asked.

'Yes,' said Dusty, 'it's the old Salters' map. Here's our hedge, and we've got to sail all the way down this river,' he pointed to a wiggly blue line, 'to the sea!'

On the bank a small crowd of mice had gathered to see them off.

'Will they be all right?' asked Mrs Apple anxiously. 'Dusty's never sailed so far before.'

'Look, my dear,' said Mr Apple, 'if the sea mice can manage to get the salt all the way up to us, I'm sure Dusty can sail downstream to fetch it.'

'I can't think why we've run out,' said Mrs Apple. 'It's never happened before. Perhaps I shouldn't have salted all those walnuts.'

'Stop worrying,' said Mr Apple. 'Look, they're about to leave.'

'All aboard?' called Dusty. He hoisted the sail, cast off and turned the *Periwinkle* into the current. The voyage was about to begin.

The fresh breeze took them quickly downstream. Primrose and Wilfred stood by the rail and waved until everyone was out of sight, and then ran to explore the boat.

They each chose a bunk, Primrose the top one, Wilfred the one below, and stowed away their toys and clothes. Then they hurried back up to help Dusty with the sails.

Poppy prepared a picnic lunch, which they ate on deck, watching the trees and riverbanks as they passed by.

'The wind's getting up,' said Dusty, as he cleared away, 'make sure that everything's secure.' At that moment the boat began to heel to one side, and an apple bounced to the floor.

'Can I steer?' Wilfred asked.

'Not in this wind, old chap.'

'We're going rather fast,' said Poppy.

'Yes, we'll be there in no time,' said Dusty cheerfully, hauling in on the ropes.

All afternoon the boat sped along, past rushes, trees and fields.

'Look out for a sheltered spot where we can moor up for the night,' said Dusty. 'I don't like the look of that sky.'

'Will this do?' asked Poppy as they rounded a bend in the stream. Dusty turned the *Periwinkle* in towards the bank, and Poppy threw a rope around a twisted root to make it fast.

They were all glad to go below deck to get warm. Poppy lit the lamps, and heated some soup on the stove.

After supper, they sat round the table telling stories and singing songs until it was time for bed. The children, tired after all the fresh air, snuggled happily into their bunks. Outside, the water lapped the sides of the boat, and rocked them gently to sleep.

Next morning, Primrose woke to the sound of the wind rushing through the willows on the bank. Poppy was already up, making toast. Dusty and Wilfred were at the chart table, studying the map.

'You'll need to dress warmly today,' said Poppy.

Soon the sails were up and they were on their way again. Wilfred helped Dusty on deck, and Primrose looked out for landmarks for Poppy to find on the map.

The day went quickly as the boat skimmed along down the river. By teatime the children had decided to become explorers.

'Look out! Sea Weasels!' shouted Wilfred.

He jumped into the cockpit, tripped over a rope and knocked the tiller from Dusty's paw. Dusty grabbed for it, but too late – the boat swung round and headed for the bank. There was a dreadful scraping noise and the boat stopped dead. They had run aground.

'We'll *never* get to the sea now,' wailed Primrose. Wilfred hung his head; he felt close to tears.

'Sorry, Dusty,' he muttered.

'We won't get off this evening,' sighed Dusty, trying to lever the boat away with an oar. 'We'd better go below and have supper.'

The sound of heavy rain greeted the mice next morning. When Dusty looked through the porthole, he saw that the water level had risen during the night and floated them clear.

'Hooray,' he shouted, and dashed up on deck to take the tiller. 'Fetch the map; I think we're nearly there.'

Primrose pointed ahead. 'Look, that must be Seagull Rock. I can see some boats.'

As they drew closer, they saw some water shrews fishing on the bank.

Dusty cupped his paws. 'Are we on course for Sandy Bay?' he called.

'Best anchor here and take the path up to the cliffs,' said the water shrew.

Dusty moored up neatly between the other

boats and the four mice stepped ashore. Slowly they made their way up the steep path through the pine trees.

At last they stepped up to the very brow of the hill, and there, spread out before them, glittering in the afternoon sun, was . . . the sea.

'It's so big!' gasped Primrose.

'And so blue!' added Wilfred.

One after another, clutching at tufts of marram grass for support, they slithered down the path.

'Which way now?' asked Primrose.

Dusty looked at the map. 'To the right,' he said, 'past the sea campions.'

Poppy was the first one to catch sight of a group of mice sitting by a door in the sandy cliffs.

'Excuse me,' she called, 'we're looking for Purslane Saltapple.'

'Well, that's me!' replied one of the mice.

Dusty, delighted, ran to shake his paw. 'We're from Brambly Hedge,' he explained. 'We've run out of salt.'

'Then it's a fair wind that blew you here,' said Purslane. 'Let me introduce my wife, Thrift, and our children, Pebble, Shell and baby Shrimp.'

'You must be exhausted,' said Thrift. 'Come inside, do, and make yourselves comfortable. I expect you'd like to wash your paws.'

She led them down a passage to the bathroom. 'This is the water for washing,' she said, pointing to a pitcher on the floor. 'If you'd like a drink, come along to the kitchen.'

Poppy and Dusty's bedroom looked straight on to the sea. Primrose and Wilfred were to sleep in the nursery.

Poppy left them to unpack and went to find Thrift. She was busy in the kitchen, rinsing some brown fronds in a colander.

'Have you ever tasted seaweed?' she asked.

'No,' Poppy replied, 'but I'm sure it will be very interesting to try it.'

Soon they were sitting round the table, and trying their first taste of seaside food.

'What's this?' asked Wilfred warily, prodding the pile of vegetables on his plate.

'Marsh samphire, of course,' said Pebble.

'Do I have to eat it?' whispered Wilfred.

Poppy coughed and quickly asked, 'How long have the Saltapples been here, Purslane?'

71

'Our family has lived in this dune for generations. A long, long time ago our ancestors left the Green Fields and settled here. We've never been back, and I've often wondered what it's like.'

At this, they began to tell each other about their very different lives in the hedgerow and by the sea.

'I've brought you a few things from Brambly Hedge,' said Poppy, fetching her basket. Mrs Apple's honeycakes and strawberry jelly tasted strangely sweet to the Sea Mice, and the candied violets had to be put out of the baby's reach.

'Bedtime, children,' said Thrift. 'If it's fine, we'll go to the beach tomorrow.'

As soon as they were up, the children wanted to go straight to the sea.

'You'd better wear sunhats,' said Thrift. 'It's going to be hot. We'll take a picnic and spend the day there.'

While Pebble and Wilfred built a sand palace, Shell and Primrose hunted for treasure in the rock pools, and Shrimp raced along the shore, getting in everyone's way.

The grown-ups spread out the picnic cloth, and reminisced about friends and relations as they watched the children play.

Suddenly, Poppy noticed that the waves were starting to creep up the beach, and she called the children back to the dune.

'It's the tide,' explained Purslane. 'It goes out and comes in twice every day. Soon the beach will be covered with water. It's time to go home.'

On the third day, Wilfred woke to see dark

clouds rolling in over the sea. Purslane hurried past the nursery door, pulling on his waterproofs.

'I've got to get the salt pans covered before the storm breaks,' he cried. 'Come and help!'

They ran through a tunnel to the back of the dune and out into the rising wind. Purslane paused to hoist up a red flag, and they scrambled down through the rough grass to the salt marsh. Wilfred could see two huge dishes in the ground. One of them was covered and the other open to the sky.

Purslane ran to release a lever and struggled to push the cover from one dish to the other.

'What's in here?' shouted Wilfred.

'We put seawater in one pan,' said Purslane, 'the sun dries up the water and leaves the salt for us to collect. The other one is to catch rainwater for us to drink.'

Just as they finished lashing down the cover, the rain swept in from the sea. By the time they got home, huge waves were crashing on to the beach, and spray spattered against the windows.

It was dark inside the house. Thrift lit the fire in the nursery and trimmed the lamp.

'Sometimes we have to stay in for days and days,' said Shell.

'Especially in the winter,' added Pebble.

The children played dominoes and five stones and made pictures with seaweed.

Pebble helped Wilfred make a little boat with real sails and rigging, and Primrose painted a beautiful stone mouse as a present for her mother.

The storm blew itself out in the night. As soon as he got up, Purslane felt the seaweed by the front door and held up his paw to check the wind.

'It's set fair for your journey home,' he said.

'Then I think we should be off as soon as we can,' said Dusty.

'We must fetch the salt up from the store,' said Purslane. 'Will three barrels be enough?'

While their parents were busy, the children went off to play hide-and-seek in the maze of tunnels under the dune. They hid in storerooms full of pungent seaweed, behind jars of pickles and roots, and heaps of glistening shells.

'Let's go down to the storm bunker,' said Pebble when he had found them all. He led them to some cold dark rooms deep in the heart of the dune.

'We come down here when it gets really rough,' said Shell. 'It's safer.'

'Where are you?' called Thrift faintly. 'It's time to leave.'

Reluctantly, Primrose and Wilfred went to the nursery to collect their things. Wilfred tied his boat to his haversack and put his collection of stones in his pocket. Primrose stood and gazed out of the window. 'I don't want to go home,' she said.

'We've a present for you,' said Pebble quickly. 'This is your special shell. Every time you hold it to your ear, you'll hear the sound of the sea and that will remind you to come and see us again.'

Dusty and Purslane loaded the barrels of

salt on to a handcart, and laden down with luggage and gifts, the little party set off along the dune.

They scrambled down the cliff path to the *Periwinkle* and with some difficulty loaded everything on board.

'Keep that salt dry, mind,' said Purslane.

'Try and visit us one day,' said Poppy. 'We'd like to show you Brambly Hedge.'

'All aboard!' called Dusty.

'And no stowaways,' added Poppy, lifting Shrimp out of a basket.

They hugged their new friends goodbye, and thanked them for all their help. Poppy loosened the mooring ropes and Dusty hoisted the sail. He steered the boat into the stream once more and Primrose and Wilfred waved until Shell and Pebble were out of sight.

'I'm a salter on the salty sea
A' sailing on the foam,
But the salter's life is the sweetest
When the sail is set for home,'

sang Wilfred as a fresh breeze caught the sails
and swept them round a bend in the river.

Sleeping Beauty

The Brothers Grimm
Retold by Alison Sage
Illustrated by Sarah Gibb

O nce upon a time there lived a king and queen who had almost everything they could possibly wish for. But neither was content, for there was one thing missing . . . they both wanted a child.

One day the queen saw a rosebud floating

in the fountain and it smelled so sweet, she put her hand in to pull it out. Just then, a bright green frog leaped out of the water and spoke to her.

'Don't be afraid,' he said. 'I have good news for you. Before long you will have a baby girl.' And he jumped back into the water with a tiny splash.

The queen was overjoyed and ran straight indoors to tell the king what had happened.

The following spring, just as the frog had promised, a beautiful little girl was born and the palace bustled with joy. The king and queen were so delighted that they decided to celebrate with a magnificent party.

'Everyone in the kingdom will be invited,' said the king, beaming with pride.

In those days it was the custom when a

royal baby was born to send out invitations to all the fairies in the realm, from the tiniest to the most powerful. Messengers were sent out all over the land.

But one fairy, who had not been seen for more than fifty years, was forgotten. And she was the oldest and most powerful of all. Her name was Malevola.

'So, they don't want *me* at the party?' she snarled. 'Well, let's see if they like my gift!'

On the day of the party, the king and queen welcomed the fairies as they arrived, and led them all into a beautiful hall full of flowers.

'The princess's name is Rosebud,' announced the king as the fairies came forward to give their magical gifts.

'Then she will be as beautiful as a rose,' said the first fairy.

'Everyone will love her,' said another.

'She will be very clever,' promised a third.

'. . . kind . . .'

'. . . graceful . . .'

'. . . lucky in love . . .'

As they went on the queen began to lose count of the wonderful gifts being showered upon little Rosebud, sleeping sweetly in her arms.

All of a sudden the air grew freezing cold, and at the entrance to the hall was Malevola hidden in shadow.

'You didn't ask me to the party, but I've come anyway!' she cried. 'And here is my gift . . . Beautiful and clever she may be, but when she is sixteen, the princess will prick her finger on a spindle and die!'

The other fairies shrieked with horror, and

the queen held her precious baby close. But Malevola had already disappeared into the night.

Just then a tiny fairy with a wand that shone like pink fire flew out of the shadows and hovered above the little princess.

'I haven't given my gift,' she said.

The queen lifted her baby up to the fairy.

'When you prick your finger, you shall not die, Rosebud,' said the fairy. 'You will fall into a deep sleep until a hundred years have passed, when a prince will wake you.'

The king and queen wept as the fairies said goodbye.

What a terrible future for their little princess.

The next day the king was determined to beat the evil spell and ordered that every spindle in his kingdom was to be burned on a huge fire.

The little fairy, who had stayed behind to keep watch over the princess, shook her head and whispered, 'What's done cannot so easily be undone!'

Years passed and the king and queen began to believe that they had outwitted Malevola.

Rosebud grew as beautiful, clever and kind as the fairies had promised. She was as graceful as a deer and so loving that no one ever wished her a moment's harm.

But the little fairy waited and watched over her with an anxious heart.

On the morning of her sixteenth birthday Rosebud woke up feeling strangely restless. She wandered from room to room, and soon found herself in a part of the palace she had never seen before. Excitedly, she climbed faster and faster up the steps of an old tower until she reached a door at the top. It opened at the lightest touch and there in front of her was a little old woman working at a spinning wheel.

Rosebud had never seen a spindle before and it seemed like magic. 'What are you doing?' she asked. 'Can I try?'

'If you like,' smiled the old woman, taking Rosebud's hand. 'Here you are!'

But as soon as Rosebud touched the spindle, the sharp needle pricked her finger and she fell at once to the ground in a deep sleep.

'See! You can't escape from my spell!' hissed the old lady, for she was Malevola in disguise. And then, triumphantly, she slipped away.

Luckily the little fairy was already searching for the princess and, warning the king and queen, hurried to the tower. There they found Rosebud fast asleep by the spinning wheel.

All day they wept and called her name, gently touching her face and rubbing her hands, but it was no use. Rosebud remained asleep, smiling prettily as though dreaming.

At last with a heavy heart the king carried Rosebud to her room, and laid her on her bed.

Then it was time for the little fairy to carry out what she had been planning ever since Malevola cast her evil spell. Gently, she touched the king and queen, who yawned and soon sank quietly into a deep sleep.

One by one, the fairy touched the cooks and the courtiers, the pages and the maids, until the whole palace was quiet except for the sound of gentle breathing. Even the cats and dogs slept, the mice in the corn and the doves in the hayloft.

Outside in the gardens the wild roses quickly began to grow and huge briars covered the walls of the palace. Days passed, weeks, months and then years. Still the palace slept deep in enchantment, encircled by a forest of wild roses.

In the outside world, a legend grew of a princess cursed by a wicked fairy. Everyone agreed that there were great treasures to be found in her palace, but that it was unlucky to go near.

Some, braver than the rest, tried to hack through the briars. But at every stroke of their swords, the thorns grew back thicker than ever until, scratched and bleeding, they gave up and slunk back home.

Almost a hundred years had passed when a young prince, whose name was Florizel, went out riding in the forest. He soon became separated from his friends and had no idea where he was until, with growing excitement, he saw that he must be near the enchanted palace of the legend. Through the trees was a vast wall of wild roses and their scent flowed around him like honey, drawing him nearer.

He jumped down from his horse and raised his sword, ready to fight his way through.

But to Florizel's amazement, the thorns melted away and the roses parted in front of him.

Soon, the huge stone walls of the palace loomed above him, overgrown with brambles and moss. Florizel saw a watchman on guard and held his breath until he heard snoring. The man was fast asleep.

Florizel crept forward, past guards in the guard chambers and horses asleep as they stood. Cooks slept in the middle of stirring their pans and children lay curled up, their toys still clutched in their hands.

As if in a dream, Florizel climbed the cobwebby stairs until he came to a door and pushed it open . . .

The most beautiful princess he had ever seen lay on the bed asleep. Florizel leaned forward and kissed her hand, and her eyes fluttered and opened.

'My prince!' she said sweetly. 'I have been dreaming about you. I knew you would come!'

And before they knew it, the prince and Rosebud were talking and laughing as if they had known each other all their lives.

Meanwhile, the palace had also woken up and everyone was getting on with whatever they had been doing when they went to sleep. The dogs were chasing the cats, the sparrows were pecking at crumbs, the stable boy was leading out the horses and the cooks were starting to get the kitchens ready for supper.

The king and queen soon discovered that the spell on their daughter had been broken and they wept tears of joy.

Not long after, it was announced that Prince Florizel and Princess Rosebud were to be married.

Everyone in the kingdom was invited to

their magnificent wedding in the palace rose garden.

Rosebud wore an exquisite silk wedding dress and as she walked by, fairies showered her with fragrant petals.

Never had she looked more beautiful than when she looked into the eyes of her handsome prince and, smiling, each said, 'I do.'

It was the happiest day of their lives and the celebrations lasted well into the night.

The prince and princess, who became known as Sleeping Beauty, lived happily ever after, forever grateful for the magic of the little fairy.

Big Beans or Little Beans?

Saviour Pirotta
Illustrated by Penny Bell

Once there was a queen who bought a giant bean.

The queen liked big things. They made her feel rich and powerful. So she gave the bean to her gardener and ordered him to sow it in the most fertile part of her garden.

'I want this bean to grow into the biggest bean tree in the world,' insisted the queen.

The gardener, whose name was Jo Lean, wasn't very keen on giant beans. In fact he wasn't very keen on giant anything. 'The beans will be too tough to eat,' he complained to the queen. 'And the tree will use up all the water in my well.'

The queen was furious. She started hopping up and down on her throne and gnashing her teeth like most spoilt queens do when they are angry.

'Get out of my palace,' she roared at the gardener. 'And don't you ever come back again or I'll have you beheaded.'

The poor gardener packed his bags and went to live with his mother on a farm. The countryside was very peaceful after the hustle and bustle of the palace. The gardener liked it. He sowed his little beans in his mother's field and waited for them to grow.

The queen sowed her giant bean herself. She grew it in a large china pot, which she kept in her courtyard where she could see it every night from her window. And she watered it with a magic potion she had bought from a passing witch at a ridiculous price. The potion was supposed to make the giant bean tree grow even bigger.

As the summer grew old, the eagles that nested in the high mountains of the land could see the farmer growing his beans at one end of the kingdom and the queen growing hers at the other end.

The queen talked to her tree to make it grow larger. But the gardener nipped the buds on his plant to make the beans stay small.

At long last the beans were ready to pick. The gardener's were rather small, but the queen's beans were the biggest anyone had ever seen.

'Hang the beans on the city walls,' demanded the queen. 'Let my enemies see what a powerful queen I am.'

The queen's servants cut down the large pods and carried them to the city walls. It took more than a hundred woodcutters chopping all at once to fell them, and more than a thousand men to carry the beans to the wall. But at last the giant beans were hung where all the world could see them.

Now, across the desert from the queen's kingdom there lived a prince whose country

was as dry as a bone after it has been licked clean. The prince was beside himself with envy when he saw the giant beans.

'It's not fair,' he screamed at his vizier. 'I want those beans for myself,' and he stamped his foot and rattled his crown like most spoilt princes do when they are angry.

The trembling vizier suggested the prince could attack the queen's city and steal the beans. The prince liked the idea. He called for his general and ordered him to prepare the army.

At sunset the prince rode out of his castle on his white horse, while his army marched before him towards the queen's kingdom.

The poor queen didn't know what to do. The soldiers in her army were too fat to fight. All those giant vegetables the queen kept feeding them had made them very flabby indeed.

'My kingdom is in danger,' wailed the queen. But there was not much that she could do.

The prince's army attacked again and again. The queen's army fought back too, but the prince had given each of his soldiers a suit of armour, so the queen's archers could not do much.

At last the queen decided to give up her giant beans. She gathered her people in front of the castle and gave them the bad news. Just then a familiar figure pushed its way through the crowds. It was Jo Lean the gardener.

'Your Majesty,' he said, 'I think I can help,' and he whispered his plan in the queen's ear.

That night Jo Lean slipped out of the city

unnoticed. While the prince's soldiers were sleeping, he tiptoed to their camp and scattered his small beans all over the ground.

Then he crept back to the city and waited.

Early the next morning, the prince ordered his soldiers to attack the queen's city again. But . . . what was that terrible noise he could hear? The prince rushed out of his tent. All around him, his soldiers were slipping on the gardener's beans. They sounded like a million tinpot kettles falling to the ground all at once. The din was quite dreadful.

'Get up and fight, you idiots,' shouted the prince.

But it was all in vain. No sooner had the soldiers picked themselves up than they would slip on another bean and yet another.

Jo Lean the gardener couldn't stop laughing.

All that dreadful clanging woke up the queen's army. 'Hooray,' shouted the soldiers as they chased the prince's army away.

The queen was quite relieved. She gave Jo Lean a nice big medal and brought him back as her gardener again. She invited his old mum to come and live in the palace, too.

Jo Lean was very proud.

'I shall grow you anything you want,' he promised the queen.

'Yes,' laughed her royal highness. 'But in the future I shall only want normal-sized vegetables. Bigger is not always better, you know.'

All the people in the court agreed.

The Mouse, the Bird
and the Sausage

The Brothers Grimm
Illustrated by Yabaewah Scott

Once upon a time a mouse, a bird, and a sausage became companions, kept house together, lived well and happily with each other, and wonderfully increased their possessions. The bird's work was to fly every day into the forest and bring back wood. The mouse had to carry water, light the fire, and lay the table, but the sausage had to cook.

He who is too well off is always longing for something new. One day, therefore, the bird met another bird, on the way, to whom it related its excellent circumstances and boasted of them. The other bird, however, called it a poor simpleton for its hard work, but said that the two at home had good times. For when the mouse had made her fire and carried her water, she went into her little room to rest until they called her to lay the cloth. The sausage stayed by the pot, saw that the food was cooking well, and, when it was nearly time for dinner, it rolled itself once or twice through the broth or vegetables and

then they were buttered, salted, and ready. When the bird came home and laid his burden down, they sat down to dinner, and after they had had their meal, they slept their fill till next morning, and that was a splendid life.

Next day the bird, prompted by the other bird, would go no more into the wood, saying that he had been servant long enough, and had been made a fool of by them, and that they must change about for once, and try to arrange it in another way. And, though the mouse and the sausage also begged most earnestly, the bird would have his way, and said it must be tried. They cast lots about it, and the lot fell on the sausage who was to carry wood, the mouse became cook, and the bird was to fetch water.

What happened? The little sausage went

out towards the wood, the little bird lit the fire, the mouse stayed by the pot and waited alone until the little sausage came home and brought wood for the next day. But the little sausage stayed so long on the road that they both feared something was amiss, and the bird flew out a little way in the air to meet it. Not far off, however, it met a dog on the road who had fallen on the poor sausage as lawful booty, and had seized and swallowed it.

The bird sadly took up the wood, flew home, and related what he had seen and heard. They were much troubled, but agreed to do their best and remain together. The bird therefore laid the cloth, and the mouse made ready the food, and wanted to dress it, and to get into the pot as the sausage used to do, and roll and creep amongst the vegetables to mix them; but before she got into the midst of them she was scalded, and lost her skin and hair and life in the attempt.

When the bird came to carry up the dinner, no cook was there. In its distress the bird threw the wood here and there, called and searched, but no cook was to be found! Owing to his carelessness the wood caught fire, so a conflagration ensued, the bird hastened to fetch water, and then the bucket dropped from his claws into the well, and he fell down with it, and could not recover himself, but had to drown there.

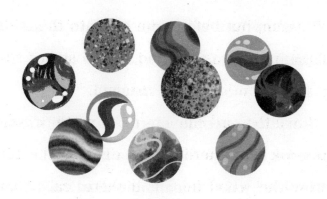

A Baby Brother *Not* for Abigail

Mary Hoffman
Illustrated by Penny Bell

Nobody asked Abigail if she wanted a baby brother, but she got one anyway. When her mother grew a bump in front of her that took up the place where her lap used to be, she told Abigail that it was going to be a new baby.

'What's wrong with your old baby?' asked Abigail, trying to fit on what was left of the lap, but her mother just laughed.

After that, people started asking if she wanted a baby brother – *or* a baby sister!

'Neither,' said Abigail, but Dad said that was rude and besides, it would upset Mum. After that, when people asked the question, Abigail just said, 'Would you like to see my Lego dungeon?' or anything to get them talking about something else.

Actually, when baby Max *did* come, it wasn't too bad. For a start, Abigail went to stay with her granny, who made toffee and all sorts of things that weren't allowed at home and who bought her a pair of roller-skates. Then, when Dad took her into the hospital, it was nice to see Mum almost her proper shape again. The baby looked quite sweet too, if you liked that sort of thing.

The best part was going into school on Monday and telling everyone about it during show and tell. No one had ever been very interested in Abigail's shows or tells, which were mainly about caterpillars and things like that. But everyone seemed to think a new baby brother was much better than a furry ginger caterpillar. And the day that Mum first brought Max to collect her in his pram . . . well! Abigail had never been so popular.

She was popular at home, too, for a while. Lots of visitors came to the house to see Max and give him presents and most of them brought something for Abigail too. 'We don't want her to feel left out, do we?' they whispered.

But after about two weeks, Abigail was totally fed up with the baby. He couldn't *do* anything and, what was worse, Mum didn't seem to be able to do anything either. She looked after Abigail, of course, made her dinners and brought her clean socks in the morning and took her to school, but she didn't play with her any more or read to her or have interesting chats. She chatted to Max instead and tickled his toes and blew raspberries on his fat neck.

Abigail began to understand what the visitors had meant about feeling left out. Not that she wanted her toes tickled, of course, but she wouldn't have minded a bit of help with her marble run. She decided to talk to Scott about it. Scott was her friend at school and he had *two* baby brothers. Well, one was a baby, born a week or two before Max, and the other was nearly three, more like a person.

'Don't you mind your mum having more babies?' Abigail asked Scott at their next playtime.

'Not really,' he said. 'I minded about Robert but it doesn't seem to matter so much about Christopher.'

'What did you mind about Robert?' asked Abigail, really interested.

'Oh, you know, all that crying and being smelly and everyone saying how sweet he was.'

'But he's not smelly now and he doesn't cry much at all,' said Abigail.

'No, he's okay now,' said Scott. 'You can play marbles with him. I suppose that's why I don't mind so much about Christopher. I know he'll be all right when he's stopped being a baby.'

'Don't you like babies, then?' asked Abigail.

'They're all right,' said Scott cautiously. 'I mean, they're all little and quite funny really. But I wouldn't want to *be* one. I'm glad I'm the eldest.'

Abigail thought about this a lot for the rest of the day and took a new look at Max when she next saw him. He *was* very little and he *did* pull some funny faces.

'I'm glad I'm not a baby,' she told her mother.

'So am I,' said her mother. 'I couldn't cope with two at once.' She gave a big yawn.

Abigail was surprised. 'Don't you like babies, Mum?' she asked.

'Oh yes, they're very sweet and little and funny, but they are such hard work and they make you so tired,' said Mum, yawning again.

'Then why did you have another one?' Abigail almost shouted.

'Because when they stop being little and funny they can talk and play and do interesting things like you. They don't stay babies for ever, you know.'

Abigail was beginning to see that this was true. Max was already looking different.

'When do you think he'll be able to play marbles?' she asked.

Her mother laughed. 'I think you'll have to wait a while for that. But I tell you what. When I've given him his next feed and put him down for a rest, *I'll* give you a game.'

This was the best offer Abigail had had since Max was born. She waited patiently while Max was fed, slurping greedily and noisily from their mother's breasts. Then she came and watched while his nappy was being changed.

'Yuck,' she said. 'How can you bear to?'

'It's all part of looking after him,' said her mother. 'He can't change his own, after all, can he? And I did all the same things for you, when you were a baby.'

Abigail had never thought of that. 'Yes, and I turned out all right, didn't I?'

Her mother laughed. 'Yes, you did, and I'm sure Max will too. But we can't wait till he's four before we love him, so I'm making a start now, just as I did with you.'

Abigail thought about herself as a baby and she was glad her mother had loved her even then. Then she thought about what it would have been like to have a big sister who didn't want her.

'I'm glad I'm the eldest,' she said, as her mother put Max down in his crib. 'And I'm going to try not to wait until he's four before I like him.'

'Fair enough,' said Mum. 'After all, Dad and I had him because we wanted another child for us, not just a brother for you. Now, how about those marbles?'

And Abigail ran off to get them.

Thieves in the Garden

Fay Sampson
Illustrated by Yabaewah Scott

Elaine had made her own bird table.

It was a big post with a flat board on top. There was a hook in the side to hang a bag of nuts on. It had been quite hard to hammer the nails in. Mum had had to help her a bit.

Her sister Janet and her brother Tom were making bird tables too. They were showing off, as usual. Their tables had little roofs over them.

'Choose a good place to put them,' Mum had said. 'Somewhere where the cats won't be able to jump up on them.'

Tom set his up by the goldfish pond. Janet put hers nearer the garden shed.

'I'm going to put mine in front of the window,' said Elaine. 'Then I can watch the birds having their food while I have mine.'

Mum gave them some bread and bacon fat, and a bag of nuts for each of them. Elaine had to stand on a chair to put the food on hers.

'Come indoors and watch what happens,' said Mum.

It was a cold day. There were not many birds about. Elaine watched and waited until it began to get dark.

'Never mind,' said Dad, when he came home to tea. 'You'll have fun watching them at breakfast time.'

As soon as she got up next morning, Elaine ran into the kitchen. She climbed up on a stool and looked out of the window. Her bird table was empty. All the food had gone. Even the bag of nuts.

'You put it too near the house. The cat must have got it,' said Janet. 'Mine's better.' But when she looked, hers was empty too. So was Tom's.

'That's funny,' said Mum. 'I shouldn't have thought a cat could have climbed up the post and got on to the table.'

They put more food out, and a dish of warm water because it was a frosty morning. A few birds flew down. They quickly ate a good breakfast.

'House sparrows,' said Tom, who always liked to know everything.

'I *know*,' said Elaine.

By bedtime there was still plenty of bird-food left. But in the morning it had all gone.

'Could it be an owl?' asked Janet. 'Stealing it in the night?'

'Owls don't eat nuts,' scoffed Tom.

'How do you know?' asked Elaine. 'You don't know everything.'

'They just don't.'

They left another lot of scraps on their tables. It snowed a bit in the night. All the food had disappeared again in the morning.

'It's not a cat,' Janet said, running in from the garden. 'There aren't any paw marks in the snow. Just some funny sort of scratches on the top of the table.'

'Let's get up early tomorrow,' Dad said. 'We'll keep very quiet and watch.'

When they woke up, nobody went down to the kitchen. They all waited, not making a sound, at Elaine's bedroom window, which looked down at the back garden.

Then Janet pointed. The tree on the other side of the wall was swaying. A branch swung up and down as something leapt on to the roof of the shed. It was thin and grey, with little pointed ears and a tail like a bush. It jumped on to Janet's table and scoffed all the crumbs. There was a shaking in the bushes. Another one leapt on to Tom's table and gobbled the food. A third one came bounding along the top of the garden fence. It sailed through the air and landed on Elaine's table. It bit open the bag of nuts and began stuffing them into its mouth as fast as it could.

'Grey squirrels!' said Tom. 'Of course!'

'The rotten thieves! They're stealing all our poor birds' food.' Janet was quite red and cross.

'It's costing me a fortune in nuts,' said Mum.

'Tell you what,' said Dad. 'Let's have a challenge. See who can think up the best idea for stopping the squirrels.'

All through breakfast the children were very quiet. They were each trying to think of a brilliant plan.

Tom went out into the garden and started pacing up and down. He seemed to be measuring the lawn. Then he pulled the post of his bird table out of the ground and hammered it into the very middle of the grass.

'I'd like to see them jump *that* far,' he grinned.

Janet was busy in the shed. She came out and fixed a net all round her table.

'The squirrels will get caught in it, but the birds will be able to fly in over the top.'

She looked very pleased with herself.

'What are you going to do, Elaine?' asked Mum.

Elaine shook her head. She couldn't think of anything. She couldn't put hers in the middle of the lawn now, because Tom's was there. And she certainly wasn't going to do the same as Janet. She wanted to think of a really special idea, but it wouldn't come.

'Elaine's a baby,' said Tom. 'Let's leave her out.'

Then Elaine turned round. She was smiling. She went up to Dad and whispered in his ear.

'Are you sure that's what you want to do?' asked Dad doubtfully.

'Yes,' she said.

He got a big piece of card.

'Right. What does it have to say?'

'Keep off, squirrels.'

Tom hooted with laughter. 'You're joking! Squirrels can't read.'

'How do you know?' shouted Elaine.

'Oh, let her do it if she likes,' said Janet. 'She won't win, will she?'

Dad helped Elaine write the words.

KEEP OFF, SQUIRRELS!

She liked the shapes of the letters, and the look of the sign in Dad's writing. She nailed it on her table, and it flapped in the wind.

The children went off to school. When they came home, some more birds had been at their table. But there was still lots of food left.

'We'll see what happens in the morning!' said Janet. 'I'm sure to win.'

'Rubbish!' said Tom. 'Mine's as safe as houses.'

Elaine didn't say anything.

They woke up next morning and raced into the garden. Janet ran to the shed and stopped in dismay. Her bird table was empty. Tom could see from the back door that his food was all gone. They all turned to look at Elaine's. She hadn't a chance with her silly notice, had she?

Tom's mouth fell open.

Two bluetits were pecking the fat Elaine had left for them. A robin flew down and snatched a crumb of bread. There was plenty of food for all the birds who wanted it.

'But that's ridiculous!' said Janet. 'Squirrels can't read!'

'You see?' Elaine smiled. 'You don't know everything!'

The Great Christmas Mix-Up

Elizabeth Laird
Illustrated by Penny Bell

One Saturday afternoon, Kevin and his mum went down the high street to do their Christmas shopping.

Kevin spotted a black leather jacket with studs on.

'Get that for Spike, Mum,' he said. 'He'd love it.'

Mum saw a soft cosy rug.

'Just right for Gran,' she said, 'when she's sitting watching telly in the evenings.'

Kevin found a blue teddy with a ribbon. It had googly eyes that wobbled when you shook it.

'Katie will like this,' said Kevin. 'She must be tired of that old fluffy rabbit of hers.'

Mum picked out a pair of slippers for Dad.

'Fully lined and going half price,' she said. 'Much better than those awful old things he wears all the time.'

'How about this for Waffles?' said Kevin, holding up a lead. 'He's chewed his old one to bits.'

'Good idea,' said Mum. 'Now, Kevin, you look at this nice pile of books for a minute. I've got something to do in the music department.'

Kevin smiled to himself. He knew what Mum was up to. She was buying a present for him and she didn't want him to watch. He looked at the books for a moment, but then something shiny on the next stand caught his eye. It was a row of kitchen utensils and right at the front, all bright and sparkling, was a lovely metal egg whisk with a scarlet handle. It was like the one he usually borrowed to make bubbles in the bath, only it was bigger, and brighter, and better.

Quick as a wink, Kevin pulled it off the hook and ran to the woman at the till.

'I want this please,' he said in a loud whisper. 'It's for my mum.'

The woman smiled at him.

'Have you got any money?' she said.

Kevin pulled some money out of his pocket.

He'd been saving up for weeks to do his Christmas shopping. The lady picked out two pound coins and one fifty pence coin and wrapped the egg whisk in a paper bag.

'There you are, dear,' she said. 'Be careful, mind, and don't get your fingers caught in it.'

On Christmas Eve, Kevin and Mum wrapped up all their Christmas presents and put them under the Christmas tree. The pile looked beautiful – all mysterious, and crackly, and exciting. They were just standing back to admire the effect when the door burst open. In came Spike and Waffles.

Suddenly, everything happened at once. Waffles saw the parcels and made a dash at them. He started chewing the paper off. Spike let out a howl and made a dash at Waffles. He knocked the Christmas tree over. Mum shrieked and grabbed the Christmas tree. She just managed to catch it in time. Kevin nearly burst into tears.

'It's all right,' said Spike, when he'd got hold of Waffles. 'Just you leave it to me. You two take Waffles off into the kitchen, and I'll clear it all up.'

When Kevin went back into the sitting room, Spike had nearly finished. He was looking very pleased with himself.

'Looks smashing, doesn't it?' he said to Kevin.

Kevin nodded. Spike was right. It did look very nice, but somehow things weren't quite the same. There was something about the Christmas tree . . . and then some of the parcels seemed to have changed shape . . .

* * *

On Christmas morning, the great moment came. Everyone gave presents to everyone else. Kevin got some Lego, and a suit of armour, and a book, and a puzzle, and a beautiful garage with cars that fitted neatly inside it. Spike got a set of new mirrors for his motorbike, Gran got a book of knitting patterns, Mum got a box of her favourite chocolates, and Dad got some funny socks.

'Here,' said Spike, when the floor was already deep in wrapping paper. 'We forgot these ones under the tree. Look, Gran, here's one for you.'

Gran quickly ripped off the paper, and pulled her present out.

'Oh!' she said. 'A leather jacket! With studs on! Just what I've always wanted. It'll keep the wind off me when I'm fishing.'

Spike got his next.

'Hey!' he said. 'What a nice little ted! Real cool eyes. It'll be my mascot. Thanks, Mum.'

Then it was Dad's turn.

'A rug!' he said, when he'd opened his present. 'Just what I need when I'm out bird-watching. I nearly froze to death last week.'

Katie had been trying to open her parcel for ages. She couldn't get the paper off. Gran had to help her.

'Nice string! Nice string!' she said, when she got the dog's lead out at last. She was so happy, she dribbled. She carefully looped it round the funnel of her train, and started pulling it round the room.

'Choo! Choo! Choo!' she said.

Waffles had helped himself to his present. Dad was the first to notice him.

'Here, that's a good idea,' he said, 'giving Waffles a pair of slippers of his own. Now perhaps he'll leave my nice old ones alone.'

Mum and Kevin looked at each other and laughed.

'I think we'd better open ours now, don't you?' she said. She got the paper off first. Inside was a cassette of pop music.

'It's a good thing we both like the same groups, isn't it, Kevin?' she said. 'This'll keep me company when I'm washing the car.'

Kevin was too happy to answer her. He was looking at the whisk, his whisk. He'd play with it in the bath that very night. It would make the biggest, the best, the most beautiful bubbles he had ever seen. And it was his very own.

Leaf Magic

Margaret Mahy
Illustrated by Yabaewah Scott

When Michael ran home from school, he heard the wind at his heels rustling like a dog in the grass. As he ran, a thought came into his mind.

I wish I had a dog. Running would be more fun with a dog.

The way home wound through a spinney of trees. It was autumn and the trees were like bonfires, burning arrows and fountains of gold. But Michael ran past without even seeing them.

'I wish I had a dog,' he said aloud, in time to his running.

The trees heard him and rustled to each other.

'A dog with a whisking tail,' Michael added.

The wind ran past him. Michael tried to whistle to it, but the wind is nobody's dog and goes only where it wants to. It threw a handful of bright and stolen leaves all over Michael and went off leaping among the trees. Michael thought for a moment that he could see its tail whisking in the grass. He brushed the leaves off his shoulders.

'An orange dog with a whisking tail,' Michael went on, making up a dog out of autumn and out of the wind.

The trees rustled again as he left them behind and came out on to the road. Patter, patter, patter. Something was following him.

'It's my dog,' Michael said, but he did not turn round, in case it wasn't.

Patter, patter, patter . . . At last Michael just *had* to look over his shoulder. A big orange leaf was following him – too big to come from any tree that Michael knew. When he stopped, the leaf stopped too. He went on again. Patter, patter, patter went the leaf, following him.

Some men working on the roadside laughed to see a leaf following a boy. Michael grew angry with the leaf and ran faster to get away from it. The faster he ran, the faster the leaf followed him, tumbling like an autumn-tinted clown head over heels in the stones along the roadside. No matter how he tacked and dodged on the way home, he could not lose the leaf. He crawled through a hedge – but the leaf flew over it light and rustling. He jumped over a creek and the leaf jumped after him. What was worse, it jumped better than he did. He was glad to get home and shut the door behind him. The leaf could not get in.

Later that evening his mother went to draw the curtains. She laughed and said, 'There's such a big autumn leaf out here on the windowsill, and it's fluttering up and down like a moth trying to get at the light. It looks as if it's alive.'

'Don't let it in,' said Michael quickly. 'I think

it's something horrible pretending to look like a leaf . . .'

He was glad when his mother pulled the curtains, but that night, when he lay in bed, something rustled and sighed on his own windowsill, and he knew it was the leaf.

Next day it followed him to school. As he sat in his lessons he saw it dancing like a flame out in the playground, waiting for him. When he went out to play, it bounced at his heels. Michael made up his mind to trap the leaf. He chased after it, but it wouldn't let itself be caught. It crouched and then flitted away. It teased him and tricked him. Michael felt that the leaf was enjoying itself thoroughly. Everybody laughed but Michael.

At last he decided he must be under some witch's spell.

I'll have to go and ask Fish and Chips about it, he thought. *He'll know what to do.*

Fish and Chips was an old whiskery man who lived in a cottage by the sea. He had built it himself. The walls were made of driftwood and fishbones and it was thatched with seaweed. Fish and Chips was not only whiskery but wise as well. He was almost a wizard really.

After school, instead of going home by the trees, Michael ran down on to the beach. He left a trail of footmarks behind him in the soft sand and the leaf skipped happily in and out of them. Once it rushed down to the sea to taste the salt water. Once it sailed up to where the sand ended and the grass began, but all the time it was really following Michael closely.

Fish and Chips was sitting at the door of

his house. Michael went right up to him, but the leaf stayed a short distance away, playing by itself and watching them.

'Ah,' said Fish and Chips, 'I see you are being haunted. Do you want me to help you?'

'Yes, please,' said Michael. 'That leaf has been following me since yesterday.'

'It must like you,' Fish and Chips remarked.

'But I don't want it,' Michael said. 'Can you catch it?'

'Oh yes, I think so,' Fish and Chips replied. 'It seems friendly and full of curiosity. Let us hide behind the door and see if it comes after us.'

They hid behind the door with the brooms, gumboots, raincoats and milk bottles all belonging to Fish and Chips. Through the crack in the door Michael could see the leaf coming closer and closer. It hesitated on the threshold of the cabin and then came in.

'Now!' said Fish and Chips, and Michael slammed the door shut while Fish and Chips jumped out and caught the leaf. Michael saw it twisting for a moment in his brown hands, as if he was holding a little fire. Then Fish and Chips opened a big box and dropped the leaf in. The lid slammed down. The big orange leaf was shut up alone in the dark.

'It won't trouble you again,' Fish and Chips told him.

'Thank you very much,' Michael said politely. 'How much do I owe you?'

'Whistle a sea chanty for me,' Fish and Chips replied. 'Whistle it into this bottle and I'll be able to use it again some time.'

So Michael whistled 'What Shall We Do with

the Drunken Sailor' into the bottle. Then Fish and Chips corked it up quickly before the tune had time to get out. As Michael left he was writing a label for it.

Michael started off home slowly across the beach. All the time he was listening to hear the rustling of the leaf behind him. He kept looking back over his shoulder. Halfway across the beach he stopped. The beach looked empty without that bright leaf tossing behind him. He thought of it shut in that dark box in the seaweed-and-fishbones cabin. How it would hate being boxed up. Suddenly he found he was missing the leaf. Michael took one more step and then he turned round and went back to Fish and Chips's cabin.

Fish and Chips was putting the bottle up on a high shelf.

'What, more leaves already?' he asked.

'Well, not actually,' Michael said in a small voice. 'I just decided I wanted the old one back after all.'

'Oh well,' said Fish and Chips. 'Often people do want them back, but they don't often get them back, not quite the same. They change, you know.'

'Change?' asked Michael.

Fish and Chips opened his box. Out jumped a big orange dog with a whisking tail.

'Like that,' said Fish and Chips.

The dog put its paws on Michael's chest and licked his face.

'My dog!' Michael cried. 'It's my dog!'

He took its paws in his hands and they danced until the fishbones rattled.

'Thank you, thank you!' Michael called to Fish and Chips.

'Don't thank me,' Fish and Chips said. 'You did it all by coming back for your leaf. That's the way with magic. But just get out of my cabin before you shake the fishbones down.'

Michael leapt out of the door and ran off along the beach. The dog came bounding after him and they set off home. As they ran under the trees, leaves fell over them like a shower of gold. The wind tried to join in the chase, but Michael and his dog were too fast for it. Trying to pretend it did not care, the wind made itself a bright scarf out of the fallen leaves and watched Michael and his autumn dog speed up the road, burrow

through the hedge, jump the creek and come home at last.

Laughing to itself, the wind leapt into a shining bush and sat there, rustling like a salamander in the heart of the fire.

The Princesses' Tears

Charles Alverson
Illustrated by Penny Bell

Once, in a land far away, lived a very poor king. His name was King Otto, and the land in his tiny domain was so barren that it grew only stones, more stones and thorn trees. His peasants were poor, his nobles were poor and even the wild beasts

152

in King Otto's royal forests were poor. It was little wonder that he was known as King Otto the Poor.

But King Otto did have three precious treasures. They were his daughters, the Princess Ruby, the Princess Sapphire and the Princess Pearl. King Otto loved these daughters well, for they were fair and good and gentle and *never* – well, almost never – complained. But they were precious to him for another reason. And it was for this reason that King Otto kept the princesses hidden high up in the tower of his tumbledown castle.

The three lovely princesses had a secret. Their secret was that whenever they cried, they didn't cry tears. They cried perfectly shaped little gemstones, rubies and sapphires and pearls, worth a great deal of money to their father. It is said that if he could have kept his daughters weeping for eight hours a day, five days a week, he would have been the richest king anywhere. But King Otto would *never* have done that. He loved the princesses too dearly, and was never happier than when he heard their laughter and songs.

However, when the royal coffers were empty, and his lords, knights and peasants were clamouring at the door, King Otto the Poor would do a very strange thing. First he would climb the ninety-nine steps up to the tower where the princesses lived all alone. This was *very* tiring. 'Ninety-seven steps, ninety-eight steps – puff – ninety-nine steps!' he counted. Then King Otto would pound on the big oak door.

'Princess Ruby,' he would shout, 'are you there?'

'Yes, Father,' Princess Ruby would answer.

'Princess Sapphire,' King Otto would demand, 'are you there?'

'Yes, Father,' would say Princess Sapphire.

'Princess Pearl,' he would finally shout, 'are *you* there?'

'Yes, Father,' Princess Pearl would say with a bit of a sigh in her voice, for she knew what was coming.

'Come near the door, daughters,' King Otto would command.

'Yes, Father.' And the daughters would come near the door.

'Are you listening, daughters?'

'Yes, Father.'

'All right, then,' King Otto would say, and

he would begin to stomp around on the little landing outside the big door making very fierce and ugly expressions and shouting through the door, 'Princess Ruby—I'll—I'll break your doll!

'Princess Sapphire—I'll—I'll throw your teddy bear out of the window!

'Princess Pearl—I'll—I'll knock all the stuffing out of your stuffed crocodile!'

King Otto could never have said this to their faces. That's why he shouted it through the door. And though the princesses knew that their father wouldn't *really* be so mean, by this time all three would be crying. And when King Otto opened the door he would find on the stone floor three little piles of precious stones – rubies, sapphires and pearls. He would kiss his daughters, gather up the gems in a leather bag and run back down the ninety-nine steps to his great hall. There he would find jewel merchants waiting to buy these treasures, and all his subjects waiting to ask King Otto for money.

Then everything was fine for a while until the royal coffers were empty again, and King Otto would have to go through the whole business all over again: ninety-nine steps up, stomp, shout and threaten until he was blue in the face, kiss his tearful daughters, collect the gems and ninety-nine steps down again. This was such hard work that King Otto was losing weight, and some peasants called him King Otto the Skinny, but never to his face.

Things went on this way for some time – which wasn't much fun for anyone – until one day the princesses looked out from their high tower and saw three fine princes riding by on a search for princesses to marry. How very handsome the princes looked, and how much the princesses longed to be rescued!

They all waved their handkerchiefs and shouted, 'Oh, help, handsome princes! Come and save us from this tower of ninety-nine steps!' But the tower was so high that the princes couldn't hear them and kept on riding.

It looked as though they would ride right into the next kingdom, and the princesses were so sad that each cried a single tear which fell – *splash!* – and turned into a ruby, a sapphire, a pearl. Then, as one, the princesses threw the precious stones down towards the three princes.

Plink! went the ruby on the head of the first handsome prince.

Plonk! went the sapphire on the head of the second handsome prince.

Plunk! went the pearl on the head of the third handsome prince.

'I say,' said the handsome princes, 'precious gemstones!' And they looked up and saw the three princesses waving from the tower. They all fell in love immediately. Princes and princesses are like that, you know.

The three princes rode immediately to the great gate of King Otto's castle and clamoured to be let in. 'Let us in,' they demanded, 'so that we may rescue those three lovely princesses and carry them off to be our brides.'

'No!' said King Otto the Poor.

'Please?' said the princes.

'Would you take away my three precious daughters,' asked King Otto, 'and deprive me of my only treasures?'

'Yes,' said the princes, 'we think we would. We *know* we would.' For princes do that sort of thing all the time.

'Go away,' demanded King Otto, 'or I'll turn my peasants, knights and lords on you, and they'll thrash you severely.'

'Let us at them, King Otto the Poor,' cried his peasants, knights and lords.

'Yeah, we'll smash them, King Skinny!' cried a very small peasant, but everybody said, 'Sssssssshhhhhhh!'

'If we defeat your lords, knights and peasants,' asked the princes, 'can we claim your lovely daughters as our brides?'

'I suppose so,' said King Otto, for he knew the rules.

The three handsome princes rode to the peak of a very steep hill not far from King Otto's ramshackle castle and waited there very bravely while the massed ranks of King Otto's subjects, armed to the teeth, charged up the hill making very fierce noises.

But just as King Otto's peasants were nearly upon them, the first handsome prince threw a handful of copper coins down the hill, and the peasants all chased after them.

And as King Otto's knights were just about upon the princes, the second handsome prince threw a handful of silver coins down the hill, and the knights all chased after them.

Finally, as King Otto's lords were just about upon them, the third handsome prince threw a handful of gold coins down the hill, and the lords all chased after them.

There was nobody left to stop the princes but King Otto – and he was too skinny – so they dashed up the ninety-nine steps into the tower and ran ninety-nine steps down, each with a lovely princess in his arms. They jumped on their fine black chargers and rode swiftly out of King Otto's poor kingdom.

King Otto was left all alone and poorer than ever. And when his lords, knights and peasants had spent all of the princes' coins, they came back to the castle looking *very* sheepish indeed. But they knew it was no good asking King Otto for any more money, so they all went home and went to bed.

A whole year passed, and the royal coffers were so empty that their bottoms shone like mirrors, and King Otto could see his skinny face in them. There wasn't anything left. But then a trumpet sounded, and a herald clad in fine vestments demanded to see King Otto.

'What do *you* want?' asked King Otto crossly. 'I haven't any daughters left.'

But the herald didn't want a princess. He just asked King Otto to follow him to a far distant kingdom. King Otto didn't have anything else to do, so he followed the herald until they were approaching three splendid and identical palaces standing side by side. And standing in front of each one was one of his daughters with her prince. And in the arms of each princess was a fat little baby.

Each of the three princesses were crying tears of joy to see their old father again. And in front of each was a pile of rubies, sapphires or pearls much larger and finer than any they'd ever cried before. The princes gathered up these gemstones in silken bags and gave them to King Otto.

One of the princes suggested that since King Otto wasn't poor any more they ought to call him King Otto the Good. And they invited him to return once a year to collect the tears of joy wept by his three lovely daughters.

Henry and the Fruit Cake

Angela Bull
Illustrated by Yabaewah Scott

This is a story about a dog called Henry, who lived in the days before cars and buses had been invented. There were trains, as you will see, but people travelled along the roads in carts and carriages, pulled by horses. That meant houses needed a stable where horses were kept – and where a naughty dog might be sent until he was good.

Henry was a naughty dog.

When Henry was led, in disgrace, to the stable, Sophie went too.

'Leave me alone!' growled Henry.

'But I'm sorry for you. Poor Henry! Fancy being spanked, and pushed out of the kitchen,' said Sophie.

Sophie was a spaniel. She had a curly coat, floppy ears, and big brown eyes. Her soupy, sympathetic look got on Henry's nerves.

Henry was a mongrel. He had a pointed nose, and a wavy tail, and he was much bigger than Sophie. That was why he needed to eat so much. And he just couldn't say 'no' to a fruit cake, left by itself on the kitchen table.

In the stable Henry flopped down on some straw.

'Are you feeling poorly?' Sophie asked kindly.

'No,' snapped Henry.

All the same, the fruit cake had been very big. It was nice to lie still, and recover.

One end of the stable was divided into two loose boxes, where the carriage horses lived. The loose boxes were like little rooms, except that there was straw instead of carpet on the floor, and the walls only reached halfway to the ceiling.

The carriage horses raised their long noses, and peered over the walls at Henry and Sophie.

'What are you dogs doing here?' asked one horse, whose name was Bevis.

'I'm looking after Henry,' Sophie explained.

'Is he in trouble again?' asked the other horse. Her name was Beauty.

'Well—'

Sophie looked at Henry with her soupy brown eyes.

'Go on. Tell them,' growled Henry. He didn't care. He lay with his pointed nose on his paws, wishing his tummy weren't so full.

Sophie bounced up on to the loose boxes, so that she could talk in a whisper. But it was a loud whisper, and Henry could hear perfectly well.

'Little Master Charlie is coming here today, to stay with his grandfather and grandmother,' began Sophie.

'We know *that*,' interrupted Beauty.

'We're going to take the carriage to the station, to meet him,' said Bevis.

'Oh, I hope I can go too!' yapped Sophie. 'But poor Henry may not be taken now.'

Even with his eyes shut, Henry guessed that Sophie was giving him her soupy look.

'Anyway,' she went on, 'the cook made a fruit cake for Master Charlie, and left it on the kitchen table to cool. And Henry sneaked in and gobbled it all up.'

'How greedy!' said Beauty.

'How naughty!' said Bevis.

'He's very sorry,' said Sophie.

I'm not, Henry wanted to say. Though he was, a little bit.

'Won't Master Charlie be cross about not having his cake,' said Bevis.

'I'm afraid he will,' answered Sophie, in the sad, sympathetic voice that got on Henry's nerves.

'I don't suppose,' said Beauty, 'that Master Charlie will like Henry any more, now that he's eaten the fruit cake.'

'I don't suppose he will,' sighed Sophie.

And that was too much.

'G-rr-rr! Clear off, Sophie!' growled Henry.

He showed his sharp white teeth, and Sophie suddenly remembered it was time for her brushing, and skipped out of the stable.

Henry put his nose down on his paws, and groaned quietly. If he'd known the cake was for Master Charlie, he wouldn't have eaten it. He liked Charlie. It would be terrible if Charlie stopped liking him.

Charlie didn't often visit his grandparents, but when he came, it was fun. He took Henry for runs, and threw sticks and balls for him to fetch. Suppose Charlie was too cross about the cake to play with him?

Henry's nose lay heavily on his paws. He wished he'd never peeped into the kitchen, and seen that silly fruit cake.

Fred, the groom, came into the stable, and began unhooking harnesses from the wall.

'It's time to go and meet Master Charlie's train,' he said to Bevis and Beauty.

There was a slapping of leather, and a clinking of bits and buckles, but through it Henry could still hear the horses talking.

'Won't it be nice to see Master Charlie?' said Bevis.

'Yes. We'll see him. We're not naughty,' said Beauty. And her long face rose sneeringly above the wall of the loose box.

Then the horses clattered out into the yard, to be hitched up to the carriage. Henry watched them through the stable door. He saw Charlie's grandparents coming out of the house. Charlie's grandmother had Sophie on a lead. Sophie's curly coat was brushed to a beautiful glossy shine.

'I'm going to the station, Henry,' called Sophie. 'Isn't that lovely? Oh, sorry!'

'I don't care,' growled Henry.

Sophie and the grandparents climbed into the carriage, Fred picked up the reins, and the horses trotted away.

Henry shut his eyes, and fell asleep.

When he woke, he felt better. He pricked up his ears, and looked round the stable. It was time for another meal. He bounced into Beauty's loose box, and sniffed at the manger.

Oats and hay! How disgusting! What silly things horses ate.

There was a nice smell of rat, but it was coming from a hole in the wall. Even Henry's sharp nose couldn't poke very far down it.

He sighed, and flopped back on the straw. Then he remembered. Charlie was coming. Sophie and Bevis and Beauty would see him, but Henry wouldn't. He was in disgrace. *I shan't let them see that I mind about Charlie*, thought Henry. *I'll have an adventure, all by myself.*

He shut his eyes, and began making plans.

Two arms suddenly clasped themselves round his neck. He felt a kiss on his pointed nose. He looked up, and saw Charlie's smiling face.

For the first time since he ate the fruit cake, his wavy tail began to stir. It wagged and wagged.

'Oh, Henry,' said Charlie, 'I've been longing to see you! Sophie's all right, but she's rather—'

Soupy, thought Henry.

'They said you were in disgrace,' Charlie went on. 'You gobbled up a fruit cake that was specially meant for me. Oh, Henry, you *were* clever. Did you remember that I hate fruit cake?'

To be perfectly honest, Henry remarked to himself, *I didn't remember. I just saw that big brown cake on the table, and I couldn't resist it.*

He licked his lips as he thought of it.

'It was really kind of you,' said Charlie.

'You're such a nice, naughty, bad, funny, lovely dog! Come on. Let's go for a run!'

The Jungle House

Genevieve Murphy
Illustrated by Penny Bell

John never quite knew how he got there. All he could remember was standing in front of a yellow door and looking up at the sign, which said THE JUNGLE HOUSE in very large letters. He looked everywhere for a bell to ring or a knocker to knock, but he couldn't find one. *It seems a bit rude just to walk in,* he thought, *but there's nothing else I can do.* So he turned the handle and walked in through the front door.

The hall was enormous and, to John's great surprise, it was full of brightly coloured birds. They were perched on the banisters, swinging on the light, flying round the room and hopping across the floor. In the middle of the room, standing on a big table, there was a large parrot.

'Hello,' said the parrot.

'Hello,' said John, looking round the hall in amazement. 'I never expected to see birds in a house. Shouldn't you be in a cage?'

'No, *thank you,*' said the parrot. 'How would you like to spend your life in a cage?' And John had to admit that he wouldn't like it at all. He wondered whether he could persuade his mother to let him have birds flying all around the house, but somehow he didn't think so.

Then John decided he would like to explore. So he said goodbye to the birds and walked through a door into the sitting room.

Stretched out on a rug in front of the fire, he found an enormous lion.

'What an extraordinary place to find a lion,' said John.

'What's so extraordinary about it?' asked the lion.

'Nothing, I suppose,' said John, 'but what happens if someone wants to sit by the fire?'

'Don't be silly,' answered the lion, 'animals have fur coats to keep them warm. They don't need to sit by a fire.'

When he had finished speaking, the lion gave a huge yawn and, before John could answer, he was fast asleep.

So John tiptoed out of the sitting room and said hello to the birds again. 'I think you ought to be a bit quieter,' he said. 'The lion has just gone to sleep.' But the birds went on singing as loudly as ever.

So John went on to the dining room. Lying across the table, he found the most enormous elephant.

'What an extraordinary place to find an elephant,' said John.

'What's so extraordinary about it?' asked the elephant.

'Nothing, I suppose,' said John, 'but what happens if everyone wants to sit down for a meal?'

'Don't be silly,' answered the elephant, 'no one wants to eat in a dining room. It's much more fun to have a picnic in the garden.'

When he had finished speaking, the elephant gave a huge yawn and, before John could answer, he was fast asleep.

So John tiptoed out of the dining room and said to the birds, 'Please do be a little quieter. The elephant's asleep now as well.' But the birds went on singing loudly.

So John went on to the kitchen. Curled up on the draining board, he found an enormous brown bear.

'What an extraordinary place to find a bear,' said John.

'What's so extraordinary about it?' asked the bear.

'Nothing, I suppose,' said John, 'but what

happens when somebody wants to wash up the cups and saucers?'

'Don't be silly,' answered the brown bear, 'animals never bother with cups and saucers. We don't have any washing up.'

When he had finished speaking, the brown bear gave a huge yawn and, before John could answer, he was fast asleep.

So John tiptoed out of the kitchen and said to the birds, 'Really, I do think you should be a bit more considerate. The lion is asleep, and the elephant, and the brown bear.'

'They're used to the singing,' said the parrot. 'If all the birds were quiet, the animals would be woken up by the silence.'

'I've never heard of that before,' said John doubtfully. He was about to explain that his mother and father could sleep through any amount of silence, but then he realised that the parrot was fast asleep as well.

So John went upstairs to the bathroom. Sitting up in the bath, he found an enormous giraffe.

'What an extraordinary place to find a giraffe,' said John.

'What's so extraordinary about it?' asked the giraffe.

'Nothing, I suppose,' said John, 'but what happens when somebody wants a bath?'

'Don't be silly,' answered the giraffe. 'No one wants to bath in a bathroom. It's more fun to swim in the lake.'

When he had finished speaking, the giraffe gave a huge yawn and, before John could answer, he was fast asleep.

So John tiptoed out of the bathroom and

peeped over the banisters. It seemed much quieter now, because some of the other birds had joined the parrot and dropped off to sleep. *They'll soon be waking everyone up with their silence*, he thought, though he still found it very hard to believe that such a thing could happen.

John was beginning to feel very tired too, so he went on to the bedroom. Lying full stretch on the bed, he found an enormous monkey.

'What an extraordinary place to find a monkey,' said John.

'What's so extraordinary about it?' asked the monkey.

'Nothing, I suppose,' said John, 'but what happens when someone else wants to sleep?'

'Don't be silly,' answered the monkey.

'Animals don't need beds. They can curl up anywhere and go to sleep.'

When he had finished speaking, the monkey gave a huge yawn and, before John could answer, he was fast asleep.

So John tiptoed out of the bedroom. When he walked back across the landing, the house was in complete silence. All the birds were fast asleep and, when John looked at them, he felt dreadfully tired himself. He went quietly down the stairs and back into the sitting room. The lion was sitting up, rubbing his eyes with a paw and yawning.

'I hope I didn't wake you,' said John.

'Not at all,' replied the lion. 'It was the silence.'

'Ah,' said John, nodding wisely. 'I'm sorry to trouble you, Mr Lion . . .' he began.

The lion immediately sat up very straight

and said sternly, 'You should call me Your Majesty.'

'I'm sorry, Your Majesty,' said John. 'I didn't know you were a king.'

'Of course I'm a king,' said the lion. 'I'm the King of the Jungle House.'

'Well, I'm sorry to trouble you, Your Majesty,' John began again, 'but the fact is that I'm feeling very tired myself now, and I was wondering whether you could find me somewhere to sleep.'

Almost immediately, the lion stood up and gave the most tremendous roar. John was so frightened, he crawled behind a chair and covered his ears with his hands.

Then the door opened, and in walked the elephant.

'You called, Your Majesty,' he said, bowing

down very low. Then the brown bear walked in, followed by the giraffe and the monkey, and they all bowed down to the lion as well. Lastly, the parrot and all the birds flew into the room, loudly singing 'God Save the King'.

When they had finished, the lion said, 'Our young visitor is feeling tired and he would like to sleep. Who can suggest a place where he might be comfortable?'

'I don't think he'd be very comfortable on the dining-room table,' said the elephant.

'Or on the draining board,' said the brown bear.

'Or in the bath,' said the giraffe.

'Or in the—' said the monkey, but he stopped before he had finished the sentence. All the other animals had turned round to look at him, and then the monkey said, 'I think he'd be very comfortable in the bed.'

'Thank you,' said John. 'That is kind of you.'

So they all bowed and walked out of the room backwards, so that they wouldn't turn their backs on the King of the Jungle House. John went up to the bedroom and, almost as soon as he lay down, he was fast asleep.

When he woke up, it was very, very quiet.

'The silence must have woken me,' he said aloud. And he opened his eyes to find his mother laughing at him.

'Whoever heard of silence waking anyone up?' she said.

'It happens in the Jungle House,' said John.

'You've been dreaming,' said his mother.

'I suppose I have,' said John, rather sadly. Then he gave a big yawn, got out of bed, and went to the shelf where all his toy animals stood in a line. While he was looking at them, the most extraordinary thing happened – they all winked at him. First the toy lion winked, then the toy elephant, followed by the toy brown bear, the toy giraffe and the toy monkey. So what do you think John did? He winked back at them, of course.

Pockets

Judith O'Neill
Illustrated by Penny Bell

Brrrr! Brrrr! Brrrr!

Meron's grandma was sewing again. Grandma loved sewing. She made yellow curtains and red cushions to brighten up her house. She made flowery dresses for herself and stripy green pyjamas for Grandpa. She

192

made blouses and shirts and trousers and skirts for her fifteen grandchildren. But best of all, she loved making new clothes for Meron. Meron was her youngest grandchild. Meron was almost six.

Brrrr! Brrrr! Brrrr!

Grandma's sewing-machine was very old. She'd had it for fifty years. It wasn't an electric sewing machine and it didn't have a treadle to work with her feet. It had a little wheel on one side. Grandma turned the wheel with a handle. The wheel spun round very fast and the needle flew up and down.

Brrrr! Brrrr! Brrrr!

Whenever Meron heard that sound, she hoped Grandma would be making something for her. 'What are you making, Grandma?' Meron would say, climbing up high to get a better look at the sewing and trying to guess what it could be.

Grandma would smile at her and say, 'Just you wait and see! It won't be very long. I've almost finished.' And sometimes she would add, 'Then you can try it on.'

Meron didn't like waiting. 'Is it a dress, Grandma? Is it a shirt?'

'Just you wait and see!' Grandma would say with a mysterious smile.

One day, Meron came to visit Grandma all by herself. It wasn't very far. The front door was open. Meron walked straight into the house.

Brrrr! Brrrr! Brrrr!

Grandma was sewing again! Meron ran to the kitchen. Grandma was turning the handle on her machine very fast. The little wheel spun round and round. The needle flew up and down.

'What are you making, Grandma? Is it something for me?'

Grandma smiled. 'Just you wait and see! It won't be very long. I've almost finished. Then you can try it on.'

Meron climbed up on to a chair. She stared at the sewing as it ran under the needle, but she couldn't tell what Grandma was making. It was something blue. Bright, bright blue. It looked a bit like a dress but it wasn't quite a dress. It looked a bit like a shirt but it wasn't quite a shirt. It looked a bit like a coat but it wasn't quite a coat.

'What can it be?' asked Meron.

'Just you wait and see!' said Grandma with a mysterious smile.

Brrrr! Brrrr! Brrrr!

'There we are!' said Grandma, at last. 'Now you can try it on.' She held it up in her hands for Meron to see.

'What is it?' asked Meron. 'Is it a new kind of dress?'

'No, it isn't a dress,' said Grandma.

'Is it a new kind of shirt?'

'No, it isn't a shirt.'

'Then it must be a coat. A funny sort of coat.'

'No, it isn't a coat. Now put up your arms and I'll slip it right over your head.'

'On top of my dress?' asked Meron.

'Yes, on top of your dress,' said Grandma.

Meron held up her arms. Grandma pulled the wide head hole right over Meron's head.

She pushed one arm gently into one long sleeve. She pushed the other arm gently into the other long sleeve. There was elastic round the wrists.

Meron looked down. The new blue coat that wasn't really a coat hung right to the bottom of her dress. 'There aren't any buttons,' said Meron, 'so it can't be a coat.'

'No, it isn't a coat. Now, I'll tell you what it is. It's a smock!' said Grandma with a big proud smile.

'Whatever is a smock?' asked Meron.

'A smock is a very useful thing. When I was a little girl like you, I wore a smock every day. You put it on over your dress or over your jeans. It keeps you nice and clean. You can spill paint on your smock and no one will mind. You can tear holes in your smock and no one will care. You can crawl under the house or dig in the garden or climb up the tree in your smock and no one will tell you to stop. The smock will get dirty but your clothes will stay clean.'

'So it's a bit like an apron?' said Meron.

'A bit like an apron. But it's got long sleeves. And it doesn't have strings to tie at the back. So it's not quite an apron. You just slip it on over your head.'

'I think I'm a bit too old for a smock, Grandma,' said Meron. 'I'm nearly six, you know!'

'No, you're not too old. Not too old at all. Grown-up people wear smocks. Artists wear smocks when they paint. To keep themselves clean.'

'I see,' said Meron. 'I'm quite a good artist myself.'

'You are,' said Grandma. 'So I made you a smock. And I made lots of pockets. I know you like pockets. I put four on the front and two at the back.'

Meron did like pockets. She tried out all the pockets on her new blue smock. Two at the top and two at the bottom and two right round at the back. Meron put her hand down into every single pocket. She had to stretch first her right arm and then her left arm to reach all the way round to the back. They were very big pockets. There was plenty of room for her hand.

'I do like the pockets,' said Meron. 'I could put things inside them.'

'That's just what I thought,' said Grandma.

Meron looked round the kitchen. She looked up high at the shelves. She looked

down low at the floor. 'What could I put in my pockets?' she asked.

'I could give you a bun,' said Grandma.

'Thank you,' said Meron. 'In case I get hungry.'

Meron put the bun in a pocket at the bottom. 'What else could I put in my pockets?' she asked.

'I could give you a knife. A tiny little knife. It's called a pocket knife. So it's just the very thing for the pocket in your smock.'

'Thank you,' said Meron. 'In case I want to cut something.'

Meron put the knife into a top pocket. 'What else could I put in my pockets?' she asked.

'I could give you a pencil and a nice piece of paper.'

'Thank you,' said Meron. 'In case I want to draw something.'

Meron folded the paper. She put the pencil and the paper into a pocket right round at the back. She had to stretch. 'What else could I put in my pockets?' she asked.

'I could give you a button. A little white button and a needle and some thread.'

'Thank you,' said Meron. 'In case I want to sew something.'

Meron put the button and the needle and the thread into a bottom pocket. 'What else could I put in my pockets?' she asked.

'I could give you a map. It's not very big. It's a map of our town.'

'Thank you,' said Meron. 'In case I get lost.'

Meron put the map into a pocket right

round at the back. She had to stretch. 'I've still got one empty pocket. What else could I have?'

Grandma thought very hard. 'I could give you some seeds. A packet of seeds. They're tiny sunflower seeds.'

'Thank you,' said Meron. 'In case I want a garden.'

Meron put the seeds into the last pocket at the top of her smock.

'Now I'm ready for anything. I think I'll go out.'

'Don't go too far, Meron. You must stay in our street.'

Meron walked out through Grandma's front door. She walked out through the gate. She walked along the footpath. She didn't go far.

'Oh dear, oh dear!' said a lady on the footpath. A thin, thin lady with rather rumpled hair.

'Whatever's the matter?' said Meron with a smile.

'I'm afraid I've lost my way. I was looking for Nettle Street but this seems to be Violet Street.'

'I could lend you a map. A map of our town. It's just here in my pocket in my new blue smock.' Meron put her hand down into a pocket right round at the back. She had to stretch. She pulled out the map.

'Oh, thank you,' said the lady. She looked at the map. 'Now I see where I am. Nettle Street's not far. It's only round the corner. I'm so glad I met you! What a wonderful smock!' And the thin, thin lady walked off.

'Oh dear, oh dear!' said a big girl on the footpath. A great-big girl with a ribbon in her hair.

'Whatever's the matter?' said Meron with a smile.

'I'm terribly hungry. I forgot to eat my breakfast. I was in such a hurry to go out for a swim.'

'I could give you a bun. Do you think that would help you? It's just here in my pocket in my new blue smock.' Meron put her hand into a bottom pocket and she pulled out the bun.

'Thank you,' said the girl and she ate the bun quickly. 'Now I don't feel hungry. I'm so glad I met you. What a wonderful smock!' And the great-big girl ran off.

'Oh dear, oh dear!' said a schoolboy on the

footpath. A friendly freckled schoolboy in a nice new shirt.

'Whatever's the matter?' said Meron with a smile.

'I've lost a white button. A little white button. From the front of my shirt.'

'I could give you a button. A little white button. And a needle and some thread. They're just here in my pocket in my new blue smock.' Meron put her hand down into a bottom pocket. She pulled out the button. She pulled out the needle and the thread.

'It's just the right size!' said the schoolboy on the footpath. 'It won't take a minute. I can easily sew it on.'

Meron watched the boy. He sewed it very well. Soon the button was on.

'Thank you,' said the schoolboy. 'That's just

what I needed. Here's your needle back again. I'm so glad I met you. What a wonderful smock!' And the friendly freckled schoolboy skipped off.

'Oh dear, oh dear!' said an old man on the footpath. A sprightly old man with a neat white beard.

'Whatever's the matter?' said Meron with a smile.

'I thought I had some seeds. Some seeds for my garden. But now I've gone and lost them. I don't know what to do!'

'I could give you some seeds. They're tiny sunflower seeds. They're just here in my pocket in my new blue smock.' Meron put her hand into a top pocket. She pulled out the packet of tiny sunflower seeds.

'Oh, thank you!' said the man. 'I'll plant

them in my garden. I'm so glad I met you. What a wonderful smock!' And the sprightly old man hurried off.

'Woof-woof, woof-woof!' barked a white dog on the footpath. A small white dog with a long hairy coat.

'Whatever's the matter?' said Meron with a smile.

'Woof,' said the dog and he stretched up his head.

'You've got string round your neck! It's tied far too tightly! Now what could I do? I could lend you my knife. It's a tiny pocket knife. It's just here in my pocket in my new blue smock.' Meron put her hand into her top pocket. She pulled out the knife. 'Shall I cut it for you? You couldn't hold a knife.'

'Woof!' said the dog.

'Just keep quite still,' said Meron. 'It really won't hurt you.' She cut the string.

'Woof-woof!' said the dog as he moved his head quickly, and he bounded off.

Meron put the knife back into her top pocket.

'Oh dear, oh dear!' sighed a very tall policeman. A tired, worried policeman with a hot red face.

'Whatever's the matter?' said Meron with a smile.

'I thought I had some paper. Some paper and a pencil. But I think I must have lost them. And I have to write a note.'

'I could give you some paper. I could lend you my pencil. They're just here in my pocket in my new blue smock.' Meron put her hand into her very last pocket. A pocket right round at the back. Of course, she had to stretch. She took out the paper and she took out the pencil.

'Oh, thank you! Yes, thank you!' said the very tall policeman. He wrote a little note. He put it in his pocket and he gave her back the pencil. 'I'm so glad I met you. What a wonderful smock!' And the very tall policeman strode off.

Meron walked back along the footpath. She came to Grandma's gate. The front door was open. She walked straight into the house.

Brrrr! Brrrr! Brrrr!

Grandma was sewing again. Meron ran into the kitchen. Grandma was turning the handle on her machine very fast. The little wheel spun round and round. The needle flew up and down.

'What are you making, Grandma? Is it something for me?'

'Just you wait and see. It won't be very long. I've almost finished. Then you can try it on.'

And Grandma smiled her mysterious smile.

The Breeze

Robert Leeson
Illustrated by Yabaewah Scott

The Breeze was nosing around among the rocks at the foot of the hills. It played lazily with the scent of tiny, newly opened blue flowers. There was nothing else to do on an early spring morning, and the Breeze was bored.

Suddenly, from above the rocks, came a great rushing sound. The South Wind was sweeping down the hills. It moved so swiftly and blew so strongly that the Breeze was jerked up into the cold, clear sky.

'Wake up, dozy!' shouted the South Wind.

'Where are you going?' asked the Breeze.

'Where do you think, sleepy?'

'I don't know. How could I know?' answered the Breeze.

The South Wind swung round and round in a great circle till the Breeze felt quite dizzy.

'Never, but never, answer a question with a question,' puffed the South Wind. 'Just listen, little Breeze, and don't forget. The South Wind blows north, the North Wind blows south, the East Wind blows west, and the West Wind blows east.'

'It all sounds crazy to me,' said the Breeze, trying hard to stop twisting round and round.

'Not at all. When it warms up, I blow north. When it cools down, the North Wind blows south.'

'Supposing you both blow at the same time?'

'Questions, questions! Well, we don't. Because there's only one lot of air and we don't want to fight over it. And, if we did . . . well . . .'

'Well?' asked the Breeze.

'If we did there wouldn't be a hat left on a head or a leaf left on a tree or a roof left on a house in the whole wide world.'

The South Wind stopped whirling.

'I'm off. Can't wait. Long way to go. Got to see how the world's been doing this winter.'

'Can I come with you?'

'Of course you can't. It's too far.'

'How far?'

'Till I run out of puff, that's how far.'

'Can't I come?' pleaded the Breeze. 'I've never seen the world.'

'Hm,' grunted the South Wind. 'I can't stop you. Winds blow where they like. And as far as they can. You won't keep up though, you know.'

'I will,' said the Breeze. 'Wait for me, wait . . .'

But the South Wind was already on the way up, out and over the little hills and into the great wide plain with its woods and meadows and villages. Trees and houses showed up black against the white snow, but the air was clear and blue and the sun shone.

The Breeze flew after the South Wind, following the sound of laughter through the bright sky.

At first the going was good. The Breeze was left far behind, but that didn't matter. It was great just to swoop round through the empty space above the ground.

On and on and on went the Breeze, revelling in the sun's light and warmth, never noticing that the sun had moved across the sky and that it was heading downwards to the west. Little by little the sky grew darker, little by little the air grew colder.

Down below, the open countryside vanished. More and more houses crowded close together, until the ground could no longer be seen, and from the dark streets below came foul smells and clouds of gritty dust.

The Breeze was choked. The Breeze was tired and worn out. As the sun disappeared from sight, the Breeze dropped from the sky into the midst of the grey-brown buildings.

Just as it fell down to the cold, hard street below, a light came on in a house where the window stood open. The Breeze could feel the warmth and was drawn towards it. There, inside the kitchen, a woman was taking off her coat. She stood by the open window and took a deep breath as the Breeze slipped in.

'Oh, it smells like spring,' she said. Then she turned and began to put things on to the table. Very soon, the front door of the house burst open and children rushed in, shouting and laughing.

'What a draught!' said the woman. She

sounded angry. Putting down the plate of food she had in her hand, she rushed to the window and slammed it. 'Come in for your tea,' she called.

There was a clatter of shoes on the floor. *Bang* went the front door. *Bang* went the kitchen door.

The Breeze was shut out in the passage. It was quite dark, and the Breeze was all alone. It rushed up and down the staircase, moaning.

'Just listen to the wind,' said one of the children. 'You can hear it crying.'

'That's not the wind. That's the cat, wanting to come in,' answered the mother. 'Go and open the back door.'

As the back door opened, the Breeze took the chance and blew out again, straight into a small garden. Now it was dark, and there was nothing to be seen. All was still and very cold, freezing cold. The Breeze wandered up and down until the flowers in the garden border told it to go away and let them sleep.

The night was long, and it felt to the Breeze as if it would never end. But at last the light, a cold grey light, came back. White frost stood on the small patch of grass and glistened on the closed buds of the flowers.

From the sky, small snowflakes were swirling. As the Breeze woke up, they whisked round and round, dancing in the air. Then they settled gently on the ground.

From up above there came a whistling, snarling sound. Something was driving the snowflakes through the air, bending the flowers almost down to the earth.

Next moment, the Breeze was caught up and drawn high into the sky. The streets and houses, white with new snow, were left behind and the Breeze heard a sharp, cold voice say, 'Hurry, hurry, hurry!'

'Who's that?' asked the Breeze, as great gusts of air blew this way and that.

'Questions, questions, questions, always questions! I'm the North Wind. Don't hang about like you did yesterday.'

'How do you know what I did yesterday?' gasped the Breeze. 'I was following the South Wind.'

The North Wind laughed with a hard, harsh sound.

'Still half asleep, aren't you? Don't you remember? The North Wind going means the South Wind coming back.'

'Will you be the South Wind again tomorrow?'

'Wait and see, Little Breeze. Wait and see.'

Acknowledgements

The Estate of Michael Bond for 'Mr Curry's Birthday Treat' from *Paddington Races Ahead* copyright © Michael Bond 2012, first published by HarperCollins *Children's Books* in 2012; *Cinderella* by Alison Sage, copyright © HarperCollins*Publishers* Ltd 2016, first published by HarperCollins *Children's Books* in 2016; the Estate of Jill Barklem for *Sea Story* copyright © Jill Barklem 1990, first published by HarperCollins*Publishers* Ltd in 1990; *Sleeping Beauty* by Alison Sage, copyright © HarperCollins*Publishers* Ltd 2015, first published by HarperCollins *Children's Books* in 2015; *Big Beans or Little Beans* copyright © Saviour Pirotta 1991, first published by HarperCollins Young Lions in 1991; *The Mouse the Bird and the Sausage* by The Brothers Grimm; *A Baby Brother* Not *for Abigail* copyright © Mary Hoffman 1991, first published by HarperCollins Young Lions in 1991; *Thieves in the Garden* copyright © Fay Sampson 1991, first published by HarperCollins Young Lions in 1991; *The Great Christmas Mix-Up* copyright © Elizabeth Laird 1991, first published by HarperCollins Young Lions in 1991; *Leaf Magic* copyright © Margaret Mahy, first published by J. M. Dent & Sons Ltd; *The Princesses' Tears*